THE WINGED WARRIOR . . .

The man from the Upper Lands lunged
forward and to Witherwing's right in order
to avoid having the swan feathers rubbed in
his face; he had seen that trick twice now.
But Witherwing, instead of attempting to
touch the Karn, beat his wing with great force
twice, allowing him to shoot his body to the
left, at the same time twisting around behind
the forward-moving warrior to the back of
whose neck he delivered a staggering blow.
The Karn lurched away in precipitate retreat,
almost falling upon Hutt, who at that
moment appeared. The sword of Hrasp's man
was quickly poised to split the boy's skull
and Witherwing could not act quickly enough
to save him. He cried out in frustration.
But the brains of the frail white boy were
not spilled. Instead the warrior was thrown
back, his face torn by terrible strain as if the
side of his head had exploded. When the
body fell to the ground it was rigid as if frozen.
Hutt had not moved. Witherwing hoped he
would never have such a child for an enemy . . .

Witherwing

David Jarrett

WARNER BOOKS

A Warner Communications Company

ISBN 0-446-90115-6

Cover art by Frank Frazetta

Warner Books, Inc., 75 Rockefeller Plaza, New York, N.Y. 10019

 A Warner Communications Company

Printed in the United States of America

First Printing: September, 1979

10 9 8 7 6 5 4 3 2 1

To Catherine and Anne,
who heard it first.

Witherwing

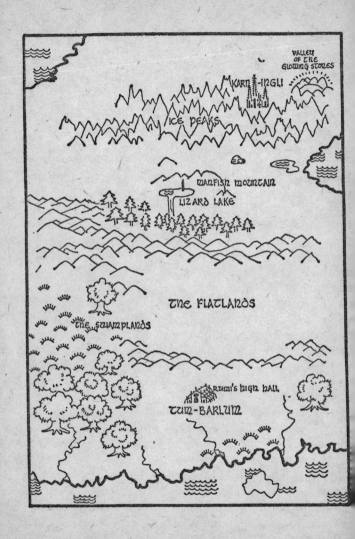

1

From one bound of the wide horizon to another where the sunset stretched a serpentine path of birds, high but icily distinct in the clear air. A musical thrumming spread over the plain below, blending notes from many different wings. Some of the birds were migrating from the approaching cold, like the arrowed specks which were swallows and swifts, or the tiny stripes of redwings. Deeper sounds beat down from the stretched-out snowy forms of geese, while rapid and powerful pumping notes drummed out from v-formations of ducks. The sinuous living line across the sky, its contours changing constantly, was not a mass migration, for there were ragged outlines of rooks diffusing far-off melancholy complaints in the air. The paddle-shaped wings of plovers flashed black and white, and, unimaginably high, strange white seabirds from beyond the Upper Lands slid along ridges of cold wind that were theirs alone.

At the edge of a dense hornbeam wood a fox had paused and raised his eyes to this great ribbon of light above him. Consequently he was late in hearing the creak of leather and sound of hooves, and a rider's lizard-crested helmet had already broken the hilltop skyline as the fox crept into the low scrub.

9

Horse and rider paused at the brow of the hill, outlined black and flat like metal pressed against the evening sky. Slowly, as if he had come far and had far still to travel, the man scanned the plain extending beneath him. It was smoky blue and peaceful, splashed with a few distant flickers of orange which were the fires of the folk of the Flatlands; from these drifted violet threads of smoke. The point from which the birds streamed was shouldered by low massy clouds drenched with pink thrown by the setting sun at the opposite quarter of the horizon. The rider lifted his eyes to the pale cold blue of the upper sky and followed the winding path of the birds' flight down to the golden flakes of the sun, whose lower half now dropped from a long purple cloud to a lemon band of light which lay along the rim of the plain.

A high singing note of beating wings, nearer than before, caught the rider's attention just as he prepared to move on. He swiftly looked up, his right hand dropping the reins and shading his eyes. More than a score of swans, much lower than the main body of birds, swept across his vision. He gazed in silence and his left arm moved inside his heavy cloak. But when the cloak was thrown back across the shoulder no arm emerged. There rose instead the feathered glory of a great white wing, which seemd to froth as it shook in the air. The wing fanned out as if in salute, and the swans wheeled, dipped and flew low over the plain, level with the eyes of the horseman on the hillside.

Witherwing watched till the flight of swans became a distant blur. Then, folding his bright wing beneath the cloak, he took up the reins and urged his horse toward the nearest fire below. The first uncertain stars began to glimmer in the still luminous sky

Witherwing, youngest of the six princes of Tum-Barlum, did not question his own legend. He accepted it as his people took all the chants of the bard, for only bardic vision could give an idea of the things that were withheld, of the mystery and doom of the world. The story was part of the lore of Tum-Barlum, and Witherwing had heard it told in the melancholy throbbing tone of the bards countless times since he had been the height of a man's thigh. It had matched the scene of its telling: The bright hall of carved wood where the flickering torchlight reddened the faces of feasted men, gleamed and was lost like a ghost in the hammered complexity of stout beams overhead where painted lizard-heads jutted down the long perspective of the roof, alternating with large-eyed warrior torsos with their hair blown stiffly back as if frozen in a clamorous storm. Beside the tall and narrow windows, shuttered against the night, had risen columns of twining serpents that seemed alive in firelight and capped by strange staring birds, their luminous wings outstretched. In such a hall of miracles it would have been hard to think of a prince's life as less than miraculous.

The bard, his eyes fixed on nothing, would begin in the elaborate word-playing verse chant of the Barlum tradition.

> See six swans in swift white flight for the sea
> Suns have been many since these who were king's
> sons
> Wore the silver lizard-mail in the king their father's
> war
> Or harried the grey wave with the mighty carved
> oar . . .

He forbore to mention that Witherwing could have been little more than a baby at the time of the

11

events he described, but that made the tale no less acceptable. It told how King Rumi had married his second queen as the ransom price demanded by the tree-dwelling forest people into whose hands he had fallen when detached from a hunting party. From the start she had been known as the Queen of Dread by her subjects, for the elusive forest folk were commonly regarded as malignant, possibly leagued with the predatory tribes of the cold Upper Lands. She was said to work enchantments through the medium of certain glowing stones in her keeping, which rendered both her and the king barren; and many had believed that the whole land of Tum-Barlum would at last be laid waste by her power.

Rumi himself had never doubted her malevolence. Before she arrived at his High Hall he had arranged for the removal of his six sons and one daughter by his previous queen to a moated tower in the isolated tract where Tum-Barlum bordered on the Flatlands. This episode Witherwing could dimly recall, though whether he was at that time already winged he did not know. He felt that his wing had always been with him, but he was ready to believe the bard's explanation.

The chanted tale would continue:

Which way the children went was known to the witch
Maid and princess her objects in magic she made
Sought them out stealthily, dealt in her deadly sort.

The Queen of Dread had coaxed her step-children—all but the daughter—from their tower and clothed them in white garments into which was woven the power of the glowing stones. So, went the story, the king's sons had been transformed into

12

wans, and the princess struck dumb from that day of terror at what she had seen from her tower. From that time she had wandered the hornbeam woods of the borderlands gathering white starwort plants which she tried to fashion into garments. A man of the Flatlands found her thus adrift and took her, though dumb, as his wife. But he was cursed with a beast-marked mother who stole to the bed of the sleeping princess after she had given birth to a son, smashed the skull of the infant and tore at its flesh like a wolf. She then smeared with blood the mouth and hands of the princess, and in the morning raged at her son about his cannibal wife. The princess, in her silence, had been defenseless. The man of the Flatlands could see no alternative to her death by burning.

As the princess was borne to the stake, she carried with her six shirts woven of starwort, all finished save for the left sleeve of the last she had been working upon. The mother-in-law had been about to kindle the fire as high as her unholy glee when the air was filled with the beating of great wings and six swans swept like gods down toward the dumb girl. Starwort and feather flashed in bright confusion, till the six brothers of the princess stood before her—whole again, but for the youngest whose shirt had been incomplete.

> So Witherwing was he called for what his sister
>   could not sew
> No arm upon his left side, but a god's wing shall he
>   know.

Such was the bard's truth.

Certainly Witherwing could remember the overpowering presence of the Queen of Dread, as he could remember awed talk of the glowing stones. Sometimes in dreams the experience of flight would come back to him too. It was effortless and his brothers were with him, but whether or not in the shape of swans he could not tell. The wooded borderland would seem to rush dizzyingly from beneath him, his moated tower growing smaller and smaller till it disappeared entirely as he flew high above the Flatlands. Always at this point in the dream the hairs at the back of his neck would rise, and with sick dread he would start to turn. His vision would fill with his stepmother's white face fixing him with glittering eyes, her thin red lips opening in a grotesque soundless laugh. Then he would awaken shuddering.

Witherwing now descended to the plain over which he had flown so often in dream.

2

Witherwing had passed from boyhood in the
years when the Horde had scraped bare the Flatlands and crossed the mountains into the borders of
Tum-Barlum itself. The Horde had come up like a
nightmare from an unknown world where the sun
rose. One day the farthest tribe of Flatlanders had
seen on the horizon at first light a black line like the
sea, and the air was filled with a murmuring menace
which steadily increased as the dark tide bore down
upon them. It was a dense chaotic mob of innumer-
able bodies without language and without leaders,
and it had begun to seethe and crush its purposeless
way over the plain, devouring everything in its path.
Individual members of the Horde were as nothing;
within the Horde there was no protection but self-
protection, so the weaker had their skulls smashed
and their bodies trampled, while the whole mindless
organism of the Horde upheld itself simply by the
staggering weight of its numbers. It could have engulfed armies; it probably had.

Rumors of the Horde's arrival and progress had
reached Tum-Barlum followed by fleeing bands of
Flatlanders who settled in outlying valleys; they had
been tolerated as long as they kept their distance.

King Rumi had taken two armed parties into the Flatlands during the first year of the Horde's invasion, hoping, if not to turn the mass back to its beginnings in the sunrise, then at least to keep it from his own country. Witherwing had been regarded as too young to be included in either of these expeditions, but when the Horde began its mountain crossing, he and many other boys attached to Tumi's High Hall were seen suddenly as men and warriors. Initially the change in status had been intoxicating, but even before he saw the Horde for himself Witherwing had intuitively gathered from his elder brothers that such war as they had fought in the Flatlands during the previous year had been disconcerting. They knew how to fight other warriors and they possessed a noble language in which to celebrate it, but to engage a sea of unarmed yet violent humanity was as estranging as it seemed hopeless.

Harand, the eldest of the princes, would not admit the Horde into what he meant by humanity. He told this to Witherwing as he placed his arm protectively, or perhaps proprietorially, on the shoulders of his young brother just after Rumi's solemn call to the warriors of his hall to protect Tum-Barlum now that the Horde had entered the mountain passes between his country and the Flatlands.

"They are just beasts, little brother, and should be treated as such. We must destroy them or fall prey to them. And now you, little one, are going to join us and help us to do that—like a man."

Harand's fingers touched lightly on the feathers on Witherwing's left side.

"Just like a man."

Harand had always cared greatly about being a man and now the first flower of youth was over in him. He was restless, gingery and strong, with a tendency to run to fat, though so far this had been kept in check by his enormous expenditure of energy. Being the eldest, he would be King, and therefore felt he must earn the right to be first in everything. This had made his ferocity in combat legendary, though legend ignored the fact that Harand lacked his father's tactical skill. It might have been the un-admitted suspicion of such lacks that caused Harand's temper to be unreliable.

"When I am king, little brother, there will be a special place for you," he went on. "Remember that. Because I want you on my side—that is, if taking sides ever becomes necessary, which it probably won't. But we must be sure to hold onto what power we have and not to neglect the opportunity to acquire more. So there will be a place for you, wing and all. And when we fight this time I'll see that you're next to me and then I'll show you how to fight."

"Thank you, brother. I shall try to learn well," said Witherwing, looking up into his brother's little eyes which characteristically darted away. The winged boy was disturbed by the tremors and pulses which ran involuntarily through the arm that Harand had thrown round his shoulders.

"And now let's get you armed," said Harand briskly. He directed Witherwing across the High Hall's forecourt and over to the armory and forge where hot metal rang under the hammer and hissed as it was tempered in water. Here was a clattering of hooves, creak of leather, snorts of horses and the laughter of men; talk that was earnest and tech-nical, equipment assessed, directions given—over all, a sense of purpose that the boy found irresistible. He forgot, for the moment, the evasiveness of Harand's small eyes, the twitch of his strong arm. And

17

soon Witherwing was dressed, like the other warriors, in tough and ornamented lizard-skin armor and a lizard-crested helmet. His wing stood out in this scene like a ceremonial cloth.

"Not so little, after all, this brother," said King Rumi as he approached Witherwing and Harand. "It is pleasing to see the eldest caring for the youngest in this way. And it may be, Harand, that this one will eventually take *us* under *his* wing." Then he added as if to himself: "There are many worse fates. Most, in fact."

Rumi was generally a distant, though not unkind figure to Witherwing; there was a cloak of melancholy around the king that isolated him. But now he tried to give to the prince some idea of what he was to meet when he set out against the Horde. He was not to expect the kind of battle he would have envisaged through bards and his own martial training and in some sense the challenge was greater than if he were marching against warriors from the Upper Lands; for, fierce though they were, they fought the same kind of battle. The Horde had no rules and little was known of its origin and nature.

"Even the bards," said King Rumi, "do not know how the Horde came into being, though I have heard it said that it is made up of the remnants of a world long since dead, a wave that still flows from some old disaster. That may be. Much of the world is a wave like that. It has been here before, though no one knows when, nor how or why it returned into the sun. But I do know that we shall not defeat it simply by fighting it. We can't fight it, we must find levers to move it away. I don't see that a wing shouldn't be every bit as good as a sword. In a world where witches give you wings there are many things that we cannot explain. But tonight you shall feast in the

18

High Hall with the warriors and in the morning you shall ride with Harand and Brandyll and Ring. And that's as good a direction as any to start searching for yourself."

Rumi then turned to his eldest son.

"Now, Harand, before feasting you and I must talk tactics."

As they walked slowly away in conference, Witherwing was struck by the contrast between his father and brother, the one calm, sad and clearsighted, the other hungry for violence as if he would run mad without it. The young prince was glad that, at least, Rumi was formulating the plan of action even if it was Harand who would lead the campaign.

Meat, drink and the songs of the bards had filled the mind with clouds of red and gold that night and these stayed with Witherwing through the gray dawn in which the warriors set off toward the mountains—at the front rode Harand, Brandyll, Ring and Witherwing. The two other princes remaining with Rumi watched the departure of the column of steaming horses with mixed emotions; they had seen the Horde in the Flatlands and they knew that the life of Tum-Barlum itself was at stake and that Harand's band seemed agonizingly small to set against what they had seen. But perhaps it would be easier to cope with the Horde in the mountains.

It wasn't, and Witherwing had known before they had travelled very far that it could not be. For Harand's generalship was torn in too many directions to be effective. He seemed to want a special relationship with everybody, like the one he had tried to build up with Witherwing before their setting out. Ring had seemed ready to be persuaded, but Brandyll was too much his own person to respond to his eldest brother's approaches except by bringing them around to a practical discussion of the present expedition, which ended by infuriating Harand. First because he felt the rebuff and, second, he sensed that his authority was being undermined. Not that it was much better if Harand encountered an admiring or yielding response—as one so forceful and energetic was bound to find often in a troop like this, for in such cases he tended to adopt a hectoring tone that was ultimately self-destructive. Witherwing was determined to stand by Harand and he recognized the importance of the initiation he was to undergo; yet before he could have found the words to express the thought, he had seen some way through authority and Harand could not provide him with a satisfactory model. But Harand had power; Witherwing thought he could almost see it lurching out of his unwilling body in the vain hope of achieving creative expression. Surely such power must be worth harnessing!

However, Witherwing had not been wholly preoccupied with such questions, for there was a pleasing novelty for him simply in bearing arms among men, in the shared hardship of the long day's ride and in the fireside companionship of their night's rest. The winged boy had fallen silent at the men's enthralling talk of women they might have had, or almost had, or, more rarely, actually *had*. But Harand did not encourage such conversation in his troop. Once, when one of the warriors had speculated about the sexual possibilities of women among the Snakeskin or Yellowmane people, Harand had flown into a rage declaring it obscene to think of sex with mutants. Witherwing had hugged his wing to himself. He had not thought of such beings as mutants, nor did many among the troop as far as he could judge by the faces he read around the fire with their downcast eyes.

Witherwing was silent, determined to learn.

When they entered the mountains that separated Tum-Barlum from the Flatlands, a dully persistent rain had begun that did not let up, day or night, until they had sighted the Horde. Though it could be only discouraging in practical terms, there was something elating in this sight that countered the wringing depression of the period of rain. For almost a day before it they had heard through the fall of water on already sodden earth other sounds, indistinct and indecipherable, as if the ground itself muttered and sighed; and then, even through all that rain, a sharp animal smell had risen to them from a valley as yet invisible. Witherwing had ridden ahead to the lip of the valley and saw first through the slanting rain that great bowl filled—unbelievably, filled—with a dark organism that he knew must be made up of individual human forms, though it was hard for the awestruck mind to accept such knowledge. It was literally a vast blot on the landscape. Those who had seen and done battle with the Horde before felt something close to Witherwing's amazement, partly because the sheer size of the body could never be less than amazing and, also, because none had seen it from above like this before. When encountered on the level the Horde seemed huge, but its extent could not be gauged—close-up, its edges did not seem like sharp boundaries, since the mass of bodies was always surrounded by vague drifts of browsers that thickened gradually toward the center.

Before nightfall the clouds began to break allowing shafts of sunlight to cut through the still rainy valley and, for a while, a rainbow arched across the dark, rumbling mass that began to steam as the sunlight struck it and the rain lightened. The rainbow brought its usual momentary wonder; but when it had disappeared, Harand's warriors were more dispirited than ever at the thought of engaging the black flow beneath them.

For several days after this sighting of the Horde there had been nothing to do but observe it and wait to see which way it would move. There were only two passes that seemed wide enough to accommodate its passage and one of these it had used already to enter the valley. Harand and Brandyll reasoned that the Horde would be unlikely to turn back the way it had come, since that would mean crossing land that it had already ravaged in the way that it was now stripping this valley. But to apply reason to this phenomenon was of limited use. All one could be sure of was that by the time it moved on the Horde would have left hardly a leaf or a blade of grass in its place. There had been false alarms. Once it had seemed that the flow had definitely started back through the pass of entry, but the movement proved indecisive and the valley filled again, while the dark mass swirled out in various directions, then settled.

Witherwing took solitary rides along the windy crests of the hills encompassing the Horde, which he came to think of as a black sea, murmuring and turbulent. He spent long vacant stretches of time staring down into the dark seeming-waters, half-wondering what might be the meaning of this for him and when he came back to himself it was sometimes with a shudder as if he had given himself up to a dangerous immersion. It was partly to break this spell that he descended to confront the Horde at close quarters. But, as he had soon realized, the body could not be confronted by an individual; for as he moved down the slopes he began to pass single figures and little groups who were part of the Horde, and there was a sense in which, as soon as he had gone by the first of them, he had entered the dark ocean that had swilled for days in his head as in the valley itself. Presumably there would come a point at which he could lose the sense of what was outside the Horde and escape would be impossible because unthinkable. At this thought Witherwing pointed his horse's head back up the Hillside. He kept his distance and no violence was offered to him by the naked Horde-members that he passed. They stared at him without curiosity and then went back to whatever they had been doing, grubbing about among the grasses, stripping small trees, picking lice from their own or each other's bodies and munching whatever they found. Or they ambled unhurriedly away from him with their stooping gait, without giving him a backward glance. They urinated and defecated as unconsciously as Witherwing's horse, which would have confirmed Harand's view of the inhumanity of the Horde. And yet Witherwing sometimes thought his horse as sensitive as any creative living and would have been as glad to accord human nature to him as to partake of horse-nature himself. After all, he perhaps already possessed something of the nature of the swan.

On one of these wanderings, as he had been making his way back to the camp, Witherwing had seen some distance below him, Harand with three or four warriors. They were in high spirits, shouting emulously at each other as they picked off with bows and arrows naked creatures at the edge of the Horde. A minor panic was created in this area by their activities, but did not last long and was never such as to interfere with their target practice. The warriors seemed not to notice the suffering they were causing in those whom they wounded, hardly any of whom were killed outright, and they continued to laugh and shout at each other when they went in a group to recover their arrows. Witherwing watched them shoot a flight of arrows high into the air so that they fell at random in the thick of the Horde and then he turned away without revealing himself to his brother and his fellows.

Toward the middle of the next day excitement ran high and camp was swiftly broken when news was brought that a definite movement of the Horde had begun through a pass much narrower than either of the two that had been looked on as possibilities. It was unfortunate that the general direction was still toward Tum-Barlum, but Harand was nevertheless delighted at the news and hurled himself into action with such ferocious energy that much of the troop seemed intoxicated by him. Witherwing savored the excitement and let it work upon him like the strange new lust that it was.

"Come, little brother! You shall be next to me in this," screamed Harand, whose wedge-shaped beard was flecked with the white of his hot mood.

Witherwing roared with the rest as they galloped to where the Horde had begun to seep from the valley.

They had stopped high above the lengthening black line that ran from the valley.

"A landslide would be the thing," Harand mused.

"Which makes it a pity that there are hardly any rocks," said Brandyll neutrally. "We could still pitch a few at them from here if you liked. We'd knock some of them on the head. But there's more of them than there are stones and we'd have dropped

24

with exhaustion long before we'd got to every stone."

Harand sensed resistance, perhaps mockery, in his brother's words and he leapt from his horse in a fury and began to hurl rocks bigger than any other man present could have raised. Soon nearly all of the troop was doing the same, bellowing the while. But the black line trickled on with only a minor clot where the rocks gradually stopped falling as the warriors spent their fury. Neither Brandyll nor Witherwing had dismounted. Harand, sweating, returned to his horse and his eyes flickered across his youngest brother as he remounted.

"Wings are not made for rock-throwing, I see," he said breathlessly. "Keep with me, little brother. Keep with me."

Sharply he reined his horse so that it reared and then plunged away with his troop in full cry behind. They continued along the ridge that looked down into the pass to which it now began to slope sharply; and after a short, wild ride they were ranged across the floor of the pass itself with the Horde advancing toward them—or, rather, with the first naked creatures coming into view, ambling toward them and then stopping with black animal stares.

Harand raised his sword and turned in his saddle to address the warriors. Witherwing had that same sense of great power choking within him, not finding the right channel.

"Warriors of Tum-Barlum, everything that you have and that you are is now at stake. If once this Horde of beasts crosses into our country then we shall thrive no better than the very grass on which you have seen them trample or tear from the ground in the valley they are leaving. Today you will fight for your life and for the lives of those you have left behind and for the life of my people . . . your people. We are few, but that will render what we do here, today, the more glorious. You are the most enviable men in the world and your names will be a power for generations. There is a flood of black evil abroad and it is given to you to stem and destroy it. But you must be bold. Hold your hand now and we are all lost. Strike, and a world is saved."

Those at the front of the Horde had by now tried to retreat, but this, of course, had been impossible with that oceanic weight of bodies surging up from behind. So they reluctantly came forward sidelong and bleating like sheep.

Brandyll leaned toward Harand and said very quietly, but urgently:

"You can't do this! Our father cannot have told you to do anything like this! Quite apart from its absolute wrongness, there is no way that it will work. This is more insane than your rock-throwing! You have seen the size of this Horde. How long do you think it would take a little line of warriors to destroy it even if these folk were to stand in orderly lines and submit willingly to be chopped? How long? You're not up against an army here. This is a nation, or a force of nature. There's not much of today left and you need days upon days and you *still* couldn't do what you want to do. Or do you just want to wade in blood?"

This last question was hoarse and accusing, but Harand was not to be reached. Some power was on him and his stillness was more terrible than his restlessness had been.

"Blood!" he echoed. "There is black blood to be spilt today. If you will save a world, if you will purify a world, then you must be at this work with me. And your deeds must shine."

Witherwing had felt the force of Brandyll's words and he knew that Rumi's tactics could have nothing to do with what Harand was leading them into. Yet he had to acknowledge, too, the somber power of his eldest brother which held most of the warriors as if in a trance. He moved forward with the rest, into the void.

There seemed to be some moments of stillness, like a breath drawn in and held while the heartbeat grows gradually louder, and then Harand's sword made a slow, silver arc in the air and he was reaping a dark harvest, swishing through the living corn of bodies like a fate. Spreading death, like dung, on the earth.

For a while Witherwing heard only the swishing of the scythe, rocking, restful. Then there came to him the real cries of men, the real turmoil of the slaughter of men, and he saw that it was his arm, too, that was cutting into this harvest and that he was no longer part of a rank of warriors, but that he was utterly alone in this dark sea of living corn where he could go only deeper till he drowned in the blood that lapped him. There were naked men, women and children showing the whites of their eyes, screaming and clambering ineffectively, yet he went on spilling the grains of this endless field, numb in the work to which Harand had led him to be a man. So far inside himself had Witherwing to flee that he could not ask "What kind of thing is a man, then?"

The rain began again and there was a swishing and swilling of water to go with the scythe and the blood. And the rain wrapped Witherwing around, utterly alone, and entered his heart where it remained like a curtain.

At last he saw through the rain a great wave that

towered over him and, cut as he might, it would not stop growing. He had become a thing of blood and his wing was deep red, for though the rain washed at it, the sea of blood splashed deeper around him. And the gray wave had become a mountain and fell upon him. And then there was the void again.

It was Harand who had plucked Witherwing from the toppling wall of bodies that had smothered him and many other warriors, not all of whom had escaped. And the King's eldest son had taken the youngest onto his horse and fled through the rainy night from the Horde. In the morning light a sorry band, dripping mud and blood, eyed each other uneasily. Harand had tried to rally them with the rhetoric of the previous day, but this could not touch the sickness of his men. So he conferred privately with Brandyll and started again.

"You have done well," he began, "and there is no cause for shame here. But we have found what we cannot do with this Horde and this knowledge will make us more effective in our next effort, for we cannot return to Tum-Barlum with our work unfinished. Therefore, instead of re-engaging this thing directly, we shall wait for it to emerge from the mountains into Tum-Barlum, where by laying trails and by prodding it, we shall simply lead it back into the hills. Brandyll agrees with my plan."

It occurred to Witherwing that Brandyll might have formulated the plan, too. But Harand had saved the life of the young prince and he did not wish to think ill of his preserver—even if, from another point of view, he was close to being his destroyer, too.

They rode away from the Horde toward more familiar country where they hunted pigrats and fished and bathed in cold rivers. There were bruises and stains of a complex kind to be washed away and generally the men did not talk of their vain attempt to cut down the Horde, though companionable conversation did return to their fires at night. Witherwing sensed that the estranging rain had entered other hearts as well as his own.

When the Horde had come to Tum-Barlum it was at first like a few stray cattle, but after two days Harand's troops saw before it a plain blackened with milling bodies. Harand himself was filled with furious disgust at the sight, but it was necessary for him to bite it back lest he lead his warriors headlong into another hopeless sea of slaughter. Fear possessed the others and Brandyll acknowledged the fear openly, hoping to channel it into a more methodical approach in dealing with the Horde, which had to be controlled from the edges rather than directly opposed. A river had been dammed and diverted, some trenches dug and banks raised, cruelly spiked with the limbs of giant thorn trees, and a trail of what would serve as food for the Horde had been laid in an arc shape from where it had spilled from the mountains. Part of the plain had been fired, which had proved one of the most laborious tasks in the mainly wet weather, and, frail as these preparations were to set against the weight of the Horde, they began to prove effective when combined with swift horseback rides that harried any part of the invasion that seemed about to move deeper into Tum-Barlum and nearer to Rumi's High Hall. The warriors began to feel more like builders and herdsmen, which proved a relief for them all. They wanted to do their work, but were not anxious to kill.

After the hunting, the swimming, conversation and hard physical labor, Witherwing found the routine into which they now fell fear-mastering. The herding rides, accompanied by whooping cries and the waving of bright banners to startle the Horde, were exhilarating; and slowly the mass was being inched back toward the hills. It had been a blessing to do something that seemed to work.

But the Horde was a whirlpool and it sucked Witherwing into its dark and disastrous center.

The young prince's horse, alarmed at something Witherwing could not see—a snake, or perhaps a scent of death—had reared and plunged into the thickening Horde. His fellow warriors streamed by on the edges, not noticing what had happened to the boy. Witherwing and his horse were not attacked straight away, but they began to be smothered and the animal soon sank leaving the prince adrift in the press. It was impossible to see what happened to the horse, for all Witherwing could discern was a dark turbulence that gradually subsided as he was borne away from the spot where he had left the horse. For a moment he was somehow raised and his wing flashed above the mob as he looked, as it were, over waves and glimpsed on the distant shore the receding figures of Ring and Brandyll trailing red banners. Then the Horde's surface sealed him over and Witherwing slipped into another mode of being.

There was no time for thought about the change. Survival was all that mattered for the moment and already fingers clutched at him from every direction, ripping his clothes in a terrifyingly short time and then starting on his wing. Swordless in a world without rules, conventions, words, identity, Witherwing had entered another kind of void and he began to claw with his one arm at the tide engulfing him. He bit, spat, kicked and was saved. Saved partly by his own fury and partly by the turning of interest away from this jerking feathered thing to the bits and pieces which had been snatched from him. Giddy and bleeding, Witherwing knew that he dare not fall, for once he was at the bottom of this ocean the weight of its waters would crush him. He looked for a way out, but there was none. All directions vanished when one entered the whirlpool. There were no names and no ways. There was movement, but no meaning. Certainly there was life, but it was life-in-death or death-in-life, a primordial swamp of endless thrashing and snapping jaws, life feeding on death, death feeding on life. Witherwing wished he were all swan so that he might fly away. But he was swampbound.

Time seemed to have stopped, too, but there did come a lessening of movement and when, for the first time, Witherwing looked up he saw a starlit sky with a crescent moon wandering across it. And briefly, for the first time, his thoughts were able to distance him from the whirlpool. If he were going to survive and escape, he realized, he would need not just the animal ferocity he had already shown, but distance and stillness like the moon and the stars. In the midst of the flailing he must cultivate these inwardly. There was violence and grunting, mating and death throughout the night, but there was sleep, too, and Witherwing was able to lie on the damp earth with only a few interruptions; he had kicked the head of a shambling man who had seemed to want to rape him or, it seemed, his wing and he had exchanged a brief spate of slaps with a woman who had wanted his sleeping space. But for a spell, amid the stench and rumble of the Horde, he was able to gaze up at the white moon which irradiated his own white wing.

Before daybreak the Horde had roused itself again and the hooting chaos of food-snatching and skull-smashing, of barging and trampling, cancelled time. Witherwing hoped he would be able to catch sight of his brothers riding by—but riding by where? For to be within the Horde was also to abolish the notion of "outside." Witherwing held on to the image of the moving moon, which he saw reflected in the crescent of his wing, and made an effort to keep some part of himself separate from the welter around him. When he had seen the Horde from the outside, in the valley and after, it had been easy to recognize the direction it took when it was on the move. But now, though movement flowed constantly around him, Witherwing was unable to sort out the general direction of the whole mass; from within all he could experience was a chaos of rebounding bodies. So he tried to build a column of stillness inside himself which would enable him to feel the flow. This was not easily done as he fought through another timeless day and then another, reduced himself at last to snatching barely edible fragments wherever he saw them, whether on the trampled ground or in a child's hand. He even thought he recognized some of the offal which he and his companions had laid as a trail for the Horde and, as a part of the Horde, he ate it, too. One part of Witherwing had grown suddenly outraged to think he was being made to follow a path by Tum-Barlum's warriors, that he was being herded into the mountains when the rich plains of his land lay before him. And if at that moment one of those warriors had been to hand Witherwing would have torn at him with the rest. He had been able to check this way of thinking, but he knew that a dangerous split was beginning to open in him. He was facing oblivion and feeling its dangerous pull.

Four times he had been rescued by night when he had thought night would never come again and then, as hunger, fatigue and sickness at how far he had fallen had brought him to the point of wishing to sink into the mud and dung at his feet, Witherwing felt a different kind of pull. He did not know what it was at first, for he was beginning to lose the language of thought, and he stood stock still as bodies jostled past him with various degrees of violence until he was knocked down. It had seemed that he was accepting the end and he stared blankly at his wing laid flat on the mud, its white crescent already soiled by passing feet. As more feet passed ovr him it suddenly came to Witherwing what he had felt—the flow of the Horde, a sense of direction.

He had built that column of stillness within him and, though he had not known it, a part of him had been able to fly beyond the Horde; now the rest of him had to follow. So the prince rose, naked and bruised, against the tide and let it sweep past him while taking care not to oppose it. In this way he planned to come out eventually at the back of the Horde. Witherwing withdrew from the struggle for food, determined not to lose himself again in the ways of the Horde; but that nearly killed him, too, for of course, there were *some* rules in the Horde and the first of these was "The weak shall be killed." By the time he had fallen back to where the press began to thin out, after how many days he could not tell, he looked like a frail seabird surrounded by predators. He had defended himself as best he could from the buffets that came to him and when at last he sank to his knees knowing that he would not be able to stand again, he knew also that he had endured long enough to pass through the Horde. Darkness had begun to fall. Nearby a solitary slouched figure beat a young girl to the ground in order to plunder a raggedly striped fragment of thorn-branch on which she had been gnawing. The girl fell face-down and lay still; she would probably perish in the cold of the night. Witherwing crawled to her and spread his wing over her back. The moon began to climb the sky and Witherwing lost consciousness.

Witherwing had woken in a mist through which no figures moved, though far away he could hear the murmur of the Horde. When his eyes opened they looked directly into the black expresssionless eyes of the girl who he sheltered beneath his warm wing. Perhaps she had been staring at him for a long time before he woke. Without shyness she raised a hand to his face and began touching him like a child, resting a finger on a bruise for a while, then poking at an eye, watching it close, then the other eye, and then a nostril slightly wrenched. The boy had not moved, except to close his eyes, because he was exhausted and strangely excited at his predicament. The dark-eyed girl with matted black hair continued to explore his face, his neck and shoulders, showing no more emotion than a fish. "They are just beasts, little brother," Harand had said, but the little brother, who had sunk into the void and come up again, had brought a deeper knowledge and he felt a blessing in those black eyes, which he returned. His wing caressed the girl's thin back and, still expressionless, she bridled like a cat, arching up her shoulders as her skin tightened. The feathers reached down as far as the back of her knees and the boy began to know what he was doing and what was being done to him when the girl's straight mouth opened as unemotionally as a door and emitted a cry as flat as that of a bird in the corn. And she raised herself like a cat while he knelt to her and continued to stroke her back with his wing. Soft white feather and tensing skin played their delicious game to-

34

gether while Witherwing and the girl slipped quickly and easily into doing what would have driven Harand into a fury. Witherwing felt himself bathed and blessed, knowing he was reaching for something to set against the void, and when his own mouth opened with a sound no more nor less human than that which the girl had made, he lifted his eyes and saw through the mist a new sky above him, more vast, mysterious and alienating than he could have thought possible before.

The girl whipped her body around, stared blankly for a moment into his face, then struck his head heavily with a stone in her right hand. Witherwing was unconscious again as she disappeared into the mist in the direction of the Horde.

The next time Witherwing had opened his eyes it was to find his brothers looking down on him. Brandyll had raised the young prince's head on his knees and was bathing his brow with cold water while Harand put a cup to Witherwing's lips and encouraged him to drink the mixture of water and wine.

"Come, little brother, taste this. Now that you've endured so much and become a man, you don't want to slip away from us again. Be strong, for we still have work to do and I want you at my side again. I will show you how we shall rid ourselves of this Horde and then I will take you back. I. . . ."

"He's been braver than all of us," said Brandyll quietly, "if he has come through the Horde. I've never heard of anyone coming out of it before. He has seen things that we have never seen."

Harand was silent for a while; clearly there were some facts that he would rather not know. He stood up and began bustling about.

"Build the fire up and bring him closer. And

then let's get some clothes on him. Come on now, at the double!"

Witherwing had refused to be an invalid. He knew that he was physically weak, but at the same time, now that he had returned to the familiar world of Tum-Barlum and his companions, he felt running through him a surge of power that he was determined to ride, even if it meant being at last brought as low as this new energy might take him high. His frailty and the trials he had undergone somehow conspired to make the solid earth seem like a vision to him and he would not willingly let go of the perception. As if in a dream he rode again with Harand's troop in a couple of days, streaming along the fringes of the Horde which was being turned inexorably back toward the hills. He carried no banner now, but let his wing open to the wind; and as he looked into the Horde, dark and deep, he was able to feel secure in the conviction that it would not touch him now. He did not look for a thin-backed girl with a straight mouth, for now he saw only a sea from which he had struggled up, and he listened with understanding to the beat and whisper of wind on wing.

A few more days and Harand, after a consultation with Brandyll, led his troop considerably in advance of the Horde until, with the mountains to the left of them, they came to a low scrubwood which stretched in front and in a horn-shape to their right.

"This is where the final turn must be made," Harand announced. "We have perhaps a day and a half before the Horde is with us again and in that time we must work as we have never done before."

Some of the warriors took to the woods where they hacked at the little trees under the direction of Brandyll. Others, under Ring, hunted for treerats and pigrats and anything else that could conceivably serve as bait for the Horde—which meant that their scope was wide—and then trails were laid back toward the approaching Horde and onward into the hills. There were others again who stayed back with the Horde to register and resist any change of direction, but happily nothing like that occurred; it had become like a huge ball rolling downhill, rolling to the curving wood and the pass into the mountains. And when it had rolled to a restless halt in the embrace of wood and mountain, horsemen galloped out from behind it dragging lines of little trees roped together and soon an arm of fire hemmed the back of the Horde. A forward impulse was generated by the flames, but this was soon checked when the wood itself took fire, raising a wall of flame that spread swiftly around the horn and cut off any passage down into the plain of Tum-Barlum. Even a drizzling rain, when it came, could not extinguish the fire; it simply added clouds of steam to the smoke and flame which penned in the Horde. The black sea boiled in panic for a while and the desperate struggle for life dealt out all manner of death before there was a pouring movement into the hills. And when the broken ring of fire had virtually emptied Harand and Witherwing led a group of warriors who plugged the entrance to the hills with trees and bushes which were soon ablaze. Then the warriors of Tum-Barlum gathered in the circle of fire, where their sweating faces shone red and gold, and laughed and beat their thighs and raced their horses in aimless circles and laughed louder.

"My kingdom is saved!" roared Harand as he jerked about in his saddle.

"We must tell our father the news," Brandyll added.

Ring poured wine down his throat until he vomited; then he began pouring more down.

Witherwing, unnoticed, rode slowly away from the group toward the fringe of fire. When he stopped and turned he saw that his fellows were still at their roaring play. He dismounted and, walking toward the flames, removed his cloak and his ill-fitting lizard-mail armor till he stood naked, washed by the drizzling rain and warmed by the fire. His body was turned to gold by water and flame. His mind was still.

The return to Rumi's High Hall had been rainy and triumphant. Harand, so long as he could be the chief among heroes, was generous in his commendation of others and he told Rumi of Brandyll's tactical skill and of Witherwing's brave growth into manhood.

"The little brother has proved himself," Harand concluded.

"He has," answered the king. "And he may have gone deeper than all of us."

This seemed an echo of Brandyll's words. Harand ignored it and went on to explain how his direct attack on the Horde had been dictated by the necessity of teaching his troop something of the nature of what they were fighting against.

There was long feasting in the Hall where torchlight played over warriors' faces and gleamed up into the colored roof-carvings while outside the rain drummed down. Witherwing listened and was still as the bard made his picture of the prince's adventure.

Hoard in your hearts the memory of this Horde
Rumi's High Hall for bright heroes makes room
Where they shall feast victors' crowns they shall wear

Knights so noble never drank through their nights
Raise eyes to theirs from which stream the sun's rays
Heard no more are the dark cries of that Herd.

The curtain of rain that had entered Wither-wing's heart was not displaced.

3

The chain of events that led to Witherwing's solitary descent to the Flatlands had begun with the arrival of a man called Hess at Rumi's High Hall. Witherwing himself was fully grown and a proven warrior, while Harand's ginger hair was peppered with gray and was thinning except where it jutted ever more aggressively from the folds of his chin. King Rumi's faculties were undiminished, but he had become more melancholy and withdrawn and it seemed that his mood had seeped through Tum-Barlum itself; all the restless energy of Harand's competitive spirit and thickening body could not dispel the gloom that had crept into the land. There was a wide-spread feeling that the Horde might return at any time, or that Hrasp-the-Hunter, the horned warrior from the Upper Lands, might cross at last into Tum-Barlum with his savage troops. Rumi's people had grown ripe for disasters and Harand was desperate to find some cure or diversion, some great deed fit for bardic celebration. When he should come to power he would need a buoyant people, for, though he was quite prepared to spend his own energies almost frantically, he always needed to feed upon others; he sought admiration and approval, despising himself for his need, which led him to various kinds of violence.

Harand's courting of Hess was one such violence.

Hess had come to Tum-Barlum alone with the air of one who was already protected. He was tall, dark-haired and clear-skinned, of indeterminate age since he looked so though he might never grow old, and he dressed in silver-buckled black leather that had been worked with a degree of sophistication that seemed supernatural to the folk of Tum-Barlum. Witherwing had been made uncomfortable by the appearance of Hess; the pale skin, thin lips and glittering eyes had started a tremor from a nightmare in the back of his mind. Rumi seemed to find something familiar in him too and he welcomed his respectfully, but without warmth. Hess did not miss it; warmth seemed foreign to his nature.

"I may perhaps have encountered some, or one, of your people before," Rumi had said to the stranger at their first meeting, "but I do not know for sure. Make my hall your own for as long as you will before you continue your journey. And when you leave, take what you will."

"You are most generous," Hess had replied with an enthusiasm that appeared coldly aesthetic. "But I think perhaps this is the end of my journey, except for the going back, that is. Not that I shall burden you for very long, but I do have some things to say to you that may be of interest. I have something approaching news for you and there are some possibilities that you might wish to explore. There may be dangerous times, you know, but equally there may be powers to be gained which will help you do more than merely overcome dangers."

"I trust you will bring no powers of glowing

41

stones into my kingdom. We have felt the force of such things before."

"They can be destructive, yes," the stranger agreed with the air of one who possessed superior knowledge. "But perhaps we might talk more of this later. For the moment I would be most gratified to have someone point out to me the main features of your great hall and its environs. I am a student of culture, you know, and a lover, a *lover* of beauty."

On hearing this, Witherwing found it hard to believe that the tall stranger could love anything. He had been watching Hess idly fingering his silver buckles and buttons and seeming to savour their fine quality; but it was almost certainly an appreciation based more on possession than on affection. Hess might appreciate Rumi and his Court as picturesque objects also. If this were the case, then Harand seemed only too ready to play the role of such an object. Hess's sharp eyes had been upon the eldest prince when he made his request to be guided round the court and before Rumi could speak, Harand, had offered his services with a characteristic mixture of fawning and self-assertion.

"Thank you, dear prince," said Hess laying a finely moulded hand on Harand's shoulder; Hess was acting as if he were the prince and the bestower of favor. "I don't want to miss a thing. Carvings, you know, architecture, legends, people—things like that I'm interested in. I hope, King Rumi, you will permit us to begin our tour?"

Witherwing wondered whether his father had registered Hess's classification of people as things. He must have recognized that the stranger was used to exercising rather than accepting authority, but there was no telling what his rank or background was, for he had not even revealed his origins, which was contrary to the conventions that governed hospitality in the Flatlands and Tum-Barlum. Rumi assumed that his guest belonged to a people in the Upper Lands with whom he was not familiar; but he was far too polished to have come from Hrasp's city of Karn-Ingli which contained the only Upper Landsmen he had ever seen.

Hess had seemed to sense what was in the king's mind, as well as his youngest son's for he turned back as he was taking his leave with Harand.

"You must forgive me!" he said ingratiatingly, but without apology. "I'm not doing my duty, am I? Not playing the game—which is wrong of me, for I love to play the game, though many have abandoned it. By which I mean to say that I should have told you my origins. Well, I have come from the Upper Lands and I shall go back there soon. And I hope that some day I shall be able to entertain a visitor from Tum-Barlum among my people. Thank you."

He still had not identified his people when he left with Harand. Nor had he spoken to Witherwing, though his suddenly narrowed eyes had been upon the winged prince as he made his parting remarks.

Rumi had spoken quietly to his youngest son as they watched Hess withdraw, his hand on Harand's shoulder again.

"I have had a queen with eyes like this man's. She talked of power, too, and had power to give wings death. It is hard for us to deal with such people, since they seem to move in other worlds. I would prefer never to have contact with them, but, as that seems impossible, it is well to remember that in some ways we cannot resist them. What we can do is resist what is unworthy in ourselves and that may save us. I saw that man's eyes on you and you may have cause to remember my words. Harand is drawn into a spell, but it may yet work for good. There is much that we cannot understand even about ourselves—perhaps most of all about ourselves."

Witherwing had not known what to reply. He sensed that some particular responsibility was being laid upon him, but the signs were difficult to read.

In the days that followed Hess showed himself in no hurry to reveal to Rumi the news or advice at which he had hinted when he first arrived. He spent most of his time with Harand, though it was clear that he looked where he wanted and saw with his own eyes. Harand began to resemble a dog that has sensed the promise of the ultimate bone and he frisked with attentive glee around his new friend. The prince took pleasure in appearing conspiratorial, in dropping dark hints to his brothers that he was the receiver of secrets that might save them all and bring great power, that he had some hard but crucial mission in which they might play a part when the time came.

"Little brother," he had said to Witherwing, who was no longer little, "even a wing may play a part in the work I have to do. Remember how I look after you when you first became a man in our fight against the Horde and be ready. Be ready. And we shall do great things. There will be a special place for you, you know that."

"Yes. I know that," Witherwing had replied. "I remember."

The signs were still hard to read, but that some responsibility was again to be laid upon him was obvious. It seemed unlikely that this coincided with the duty to which Rumi had vaguely pointed him.

"But for now, little one, I just want you to help with the entertainments that I'm putting on for our guest. I think it's important to treat him well and tactfully. He can give me . . . us, all of us, enormous power if we're careful enough. And daring enough too, of course. It's no use thinking we can get it for nothing. Anyway, he's very anxious to see some of our sports. He's really quite excited about the violent ones. I don't suppose they go in for them too much where he comes from . . ."

"Which is where?" Witherwing interrupted. "Do we know that yet?"

"From the Upper Lands, of course. He told us that straight away. Almost straight away."

"Do we know anyone who has visited and returned from the Upper Lands? Do we have any idea of the extent of the Upper Lands? I have heard of the city of Karn-Ingli, but this man Hess is no Karn."

"Damned right he's no Karn!" blustered Harand, who was not used to being questioned by Witherwing and who struck his "little brother" on the shoulder to emphasize his point. "But that doesn't mean that we're not going to have to deal with Karns, horned kings and all! And who knows if a few feathers won't come in handy in such an enterprise? Little one, I have need of you and we may gain great things through this man Hess. Trust me. I *have* to trust him."

It was hard for Witherwing to resist this appeal. He wanted to trust his brother, but the back of his neck tended to tingle when he saw the glittering eyes of Hess.

Harand threw himself into preparing sports for Hess's delectation. He saw to the erection of an enclosure for the sticking of pigrats and to a sortie into the woods to capture enough of these animals to make for a good day's killing; he had built a ring for wrestling and fighting with staves; and lists were

45

put up for the bruising horseback encounters in which the combatants struck at each other with heavy clubs as they passed. Harand had wanted swordfights, too, but King Rumi had forbidden this, as he would have liked, perhaps, to have forbidden the whole display. It was even rumored that Harand had suggested to his father that a few of the Snakeskin people of the Swamplands might be rounded up to vary the program of pigrat-sticking. But Witherwing could give no credence to such gossip.

During the three days of sport, Harand had not only acted as master of the ceremonies, but he had also waited upon Hess and participated with furious concentration in the games and contests. He did not have a young man's suppleness, but he was heavy and strong and in the grip of a will-to-power that could never leave him in peace. As he wrestled, or as he chose the fiercest pigrat to stab, or as he hammered down opponents in the lists, it seemed that the knotted veins of his neck and temples must burst, that his heart could not sustain the pressure which he placed upon it. Witherwing found it painful to see his brother operating on the dangerous edge like this, but he had to admire something in this desperate drive for domination. He felt, however, that Harand probably had little understanding of what was driving him; but Witherwing remembered the reaping of that dark and impossible harvest when, years before, Harand had insisted on facing the Horde and now he sensed that what powered the jerking vitality of the eldest prince was the love of death and, perhaps, the desire for it. He remembered Brandyll's qustion to Harand before that estranging fight against a tide of bodies:

"Or do you just want to wade in blood?"

Perhaps Harand would be happiest wading in his own.

Witherwing did not have a taste for sticking penned pigrats, though he had often enjoyed hunting them in the woods; nor, with his one arm, was he built for wrestling—and clubbing one's friends in the lists seemed a fruitless pastime to him. So he had not played a major part in the sports, but, for the sake of Harand, he had attended dutifully and had been as encouraging as he could. It had not been pleasant to witness the reactions of Hess to the entertainments that Harand had provided, for the stranger from the Upper Lands, customarily so poised and still, had squirmed and squealed in excitement at the violence. Each time that a pigrat was skewered and, perhaps, pinned wriggling to the ground he had gasped and rubbed his hands or clapped them repeatedly on his raised knees. And if one of the warriors were gored, Hess's feet drummed rapidly up and down at the thrill of it all. Though the weather was warm and trees were in blossom, Rumi generally sat beside his guest wrapped in a thick cloak which manifested his mood. Hess paid no attention to the king's gloom and expressed his titillation unashamedly.

"Oh, what a show! What a splendid game this is! I can't understand how anyone could have abandoned such a sport. I'm sure I shall never be able to get enough of it, and just think of all the new shapes it could take! We must set to work for it is time for me to reveal what I came to tell you. This is rare indeed! Just *look* at that wound! That blood, that *blood!*"

Rumi had seemed resigned, as if he knew already that revelations from such as Hess were unlikely to be either clear or beneficial to the folk of

Tum-Barlum; but he also knew that Hess could not be ignored. So after the three days of violent play, while Harand still glowed with his triumphs, the king and his guest were closeted together for many hours. Just when he was beginning to feel nervous about being excluded, Harand was called in by the king and the talk went on far into the night. By the next morning Hess had already left Rumi's High Hall, presumably to return to the Upper Lands. Rumi's sons were summoned and the still-cloaked king spoke quietly to them his head bowed and shadowed.

"My sons, as I expected, I have learnt little and been promised much that is ambiguous. My faith in the stranger who has left us is not great, but I do not think he has lied to us. He tells us that Tum-Barlum is in danger from the Upper Lands, that it will not be many years before Hrasp-the-Hunter crosses the Flatlands, which he plunders regularly, and that then he will destroy our land. But the stranger also says that this can be averted, that now is a time for heroes and for the undertaking of quests to outwit our enemies. And I see no alternative to our following—with our eyes open—where he points, for I think we *are* in danger. First, it is necessary for some of you to seek help, advice or information from the Forest Folk beyond our borders, which cannot be an easy task, since they have not served you or me well in the past. I have been a prisoner in their trees and was imprisoned in unwelcome wedlock and had you, my children, stolen from me. You are expected, but you will go armed and ready for betrayal. The Forest Folk are not to be underestimated; they do not look like warriors, are not like us, and I know them to be in touch with powers which we do not understand. Perhaps we are now to learn of these; I cannot pretend to welcome the opportunity. This is no pigrat-sticking expedition and you must not initiate violence; if you do, you will have doomed yourself and perhaps Tum-Barlum, too. Harand, who saved us from the Horde, will lead the troop with Brandyll and Witherwing. My other sons I shall keep with me."

Ring had been offended at his omission from the party—after all, he too had saved Tum-Barlum from the Horde. But Harand had taken him aside and given him earnest assurances of some sort so that he returned reconciled to the arrangement. Harand had seemed determined to lift some of the gloom which his father had thrown on the coming quest and spoke excitedly to his brothers about the greatness of the opportunities that awaited them. He had heard enough from Hess to know that there was much at stake, much to be gained, and he relied wholeheartedly on his brothers, he said, and they, of course, would be rewarded in ways that they could not conceive.

It had been a bright spring day when Harand and his companions set out for the forest. None of them had a clear idea of where they were going or why, but the season and Harand's confidence that great deeds were to be done inspired a youthful enthusiasm which persisted after they had entered the sun-dappled green aisles of the forest. Witherwing had hunted in these woods since boyhood and was well acquainted with their dangers and their beauties; he had seen a man-eating fungus swallow one of his father's men and had spent nights of pure contentment sleeping on the mossy forest floor. When once he had penetrated to where the trees began to turn into giants he had seen, or thought he had seen some of the Forest Folk; it was hard to know for sure, since they could look so much like the branches among which they lived. They had made for themselves a rookery-like treetop world in the oldest part of the forest where the branches of huge mutated trees were their highways. It was the Forest Folk, elusive as birds, who had taken Rumi prisoner years before and had thus been able to force the Queen of Dread upon Tum-Barlum. Her association with them was obscure, for she was certainly not born to the Forest Folk; her cruelly bright complexion and her lack of the Forester's rangey, sticklike physique were clear indications of this.

The woods had continued quiet and warm as the men of Tum-Barlum rode deeper into the green world and at last the silence grew tense as if there were watchers near at hand. Harand's men were prepared for this, of course, for it was known that the Forest Folk would make contact with them, and yet it grew unnerving after several days in which the sky seemed to grow progressively further from them to be replaced by thick curtains of new-sprung leaves that spread a green dusk where the warriors rode. Witherwing had been the first on this occasion to sight one of the Forest Folk and it seemed fitting that a white bird had drawn his attention to the watcher. For he had looked up to see a dove ascend from a tossing branch and disappear in and, presumably, beyond the treetops and it had been several moments before he realized that the branch was a wrist and that he was staring directly into the eyes of a bark-colored human form that scrutinized him intently. Witherwing had touched the sleeve of his brother Harand and soon the whole troop had halted and was staring silently up at the unmoving and unfrightened figure. To the men of Tum-Barlum it began to seem as if they were in a deep vault, that they were small and earthbound, perhaps even imprisoned. In the silence of that pause they gradually perceived that there were other branchlike forms of men shrouded by leaves above them, but there was no movement apart from a breath of wind in the foliage, there was no sign of recognition or welcome. Harand headed his men deeper into the shadowy woods.

Somehow Witherwing knew that he and his comrades could not miss their way, for it was as if the silent figures high in the trees were funneling Harand's troop toward its destination. The forest might seem trackless, but a path could be traced by following the line, sometimes seen, sometimes more ambiguously sensed, in which the Forest Folk appeared to have arranged themselves. As the men of Tum-Barlum progressed the trees grew vaster and sunlight found it harder to filter through to the forest floor. Convolutions of muscular roots took on fantastic shapes in the gloom and there could have been few warriors who did not fancy from time to time that some twisted branch was reaching out for him. There were unfamiliar cries and grunts from the undergrowth, rendered ghostly by the huge surrounding silence; unseen beasts crept near the men and then slipped away, still unseen; ominous burblings issued from the fungi which were draped like enormous lungs down the trunks of some of the trees. At this level of the forest there were no birds. This was literally the underworld, a vale of shadows. Sense of time was loosened and, with it, the sense of identity.

But a clearing was reached at last where the sky could be seen again. Witherwing and his companions felt as if they stood at the bottom of a gigantic circular tower open at the top and their eyes and spirits rushed hungrily to the disc of blue sky. It was not until he spoke that the warriors noticed that one of the Forest Folk stood in the center of the clearing; and even then they were not altogether sure, for the body might almost have been a small leafless tree and the voice might have been the grating of two dry branches in the wind.

"Welcome," creaked the knotted body a second time.

Harand, though leader of the troop, was unable to respond. He jerked his head from side to side as if in disbelief and his mouth fell open though he could not force a sound from it. Eventually he managed a squeak which was much less comprehensible than the Forester's greeting, but by that time Brandyll had dismounted, taken the twiglike fingers in his own and returned the courtesy of the Forester whom he then led over to Harand. The Prince fluttered his own hand near the Forester's in a noncommittal way and twitched a nod or bow in his general direction; but he did not get down from his horse.

"Your horses will be cared for, have no fear," said the Forester whose brown body was adorned with an inscrutable arrangement of black rags like a crow's wing in a high wind. "It is best that you dismount here so that you may be properly received."

The Forester made a gesture toward the distant treetops.

"Most kind. Yes. Received, um . . . ."

Brandyll signalled to the men to get down from their horses since Harand seemed still at a loss. No sooner had the warriors' feet touched the ground than groups of hitherto unseen Forest Folk glided down from the trees and quietly led away the horses which were given up to them at a nod from Brandyll. Harand was the last to surrender his mount, but he did it at last with a dreamlike reluctance and then walked stiffly with his host toward the trees. Brandyll and Witherwing fell in behind him, knowing the onus of this reception might fall on them; neither wanted to undermine or shame his eldest brother. When they reached the foot of a giant tree Harand threw his head wildly around to his brothers and his whispered words came like a rush of steam.

"I can't deal with twigs or insects! What can I learn from them? What kind of power can these brittle bits of nothing have? I'm a man, a *man*, and I want to deal with men! Hess didn't tell me that they were like this, these *things!*"

"Hess wasn't above calling *us* things either," Witherwing snapped back at his brother, and he was surprised at his own vehemence. "And these folk have held a king of Tum-Barlum to ransom, remember."

Witherwing had instinctively said the right thing in the right tone and Harand struggled to lose his dignity no further as he entered, with his warriors, a new world. The men of Tum-Barlum probably thought of tree-climbing as a boyish activity, but the ascent which they now undertook did not involve simply hauling oneself from branch to branch, balancing precariously and clinging to bending boughs. Rather it was as if they had entered an ancient castle of huge extent and complexity. Steps wound up and through towering trunks and there were bridges of flat-topped boughs that took four men abreast and still left room for someone to pass in the opposite direction. All kinds of semi-organic structures—halls, nests, chambers—passed before their gaze as they moved higher up this tree-world. Harand had gradually won control of himself, though

53

he could not resist turning to his brothers as more and more Forest Folk came into view and saying:

"I'll never tell them apart. They're all the same to me. How am I supposed to tell one bit of twig from another?"

Even Witherwing had to admit inwardly that this was a real difficulty. He had thought that the black rags which flapped around their guide might be a badge of office and that such things would help him to distinguish between different Forest Folk, but it seemed that they all wore rags like this. Witherwing could not discern any kind of system in this clothing—if clothing it was; perhaps, he thought, it's a kind of feathered growth.

At about the height of a normal tree from the top of the forest they came to a floor woven of living branches where stood a great concourse of the Forest Folk like a brown wood-within-a-wood. Hooded crows with gray beaks wheeled and hopped unmolested around, alighting indiscriminately on branches or on the Forest Folk, while, just above the treetops, a flock of white birds flashed in the sunlight, circled the assembly, and then settled in the highest branches. The guide motioned the warriors to a long, low bough that would serve as a seat. They did as directed and waited for some further ceremony; but nothing happened. The group of Forest Folk remained before them, swaying slightly, just like wood, and there were creaking noises which may have been speech among the Foresters or just the sounds made by weight on the woven floor. Time passed and still nothing happened. Except that the men of Tum-Barlum began to pay closer attention to the brown swaying bodies, beginning to wonder whether the movements were concerted, and gradually it dawned upon them that here was the subtlest of dances. The longer one looked, the more significant seemed each slight movement and Witherwing, entranced at seeing, as it were, the woods get up and dance, also began to hear them sing the subtlest of songs. First the music crept into his senses, changing from a creak to a hum to a harmony, and then followed words and meaning, though, right through the performance, the winged prince remained uncertain of how much of that meaning he was supplying.

> *There's makers and masters*
> > *And Time upon Time.*
> *There's change and disasters*
> > *And Time and more Time.*

> *There's masters and players*
> > *And Time and the Game.*
> *There's no place for prayers*
> > *To the Masters of Game.*

> *There's death and forgetting*
> > *And ends, but no end.*
> *And still there is fretting*
> > *After the end.*

This did not appear to Witherwing an auspicious welcome, but he had not nursed expectations of warm greetings from the people who had kidnapped his father and given the princes a stepmother out of nightmare; as it were, he found this ritual strangely moving. He could not tell what the others were making of it, but when he looked at Harand he saw only blank incomprehension.

> *There's masters and makers*
> > *There's horn and there's wing*

55

There's blood and there's battle
For poets to sing.

Before nightfall the little group of warriors was fed with unfamiliar food and drink and there were stiff and slow exchanges between hosts and guests. It was a relief to everybody when they retired, Harand and his men being shown to what seemed at first to be a line of stick-piles, but which turned out to be a series of relatively comfortable chambers. Before they fell asleep the men of Tum-Barlum realized that this treetop world was in constant motion, swaying considerable distances from side to side.

In the morning there was more food, more awkward, formal conversation between parties who had to strain to understand every word, more swaying dance and song, conveying strange messages that were, perhaps, different for every listener, and then a Forester who might have been their guide of the previous day stepped forward and said:

"The old one wishes to see the one with the wing."

"What did it say? What did it say?" hissed Harand at his brothers.

"The old one has words for the redbeard later," the Forester added, stepping over to Witherwing and indicating that he should follow.

Witherwing went with him along a wooden path through thick foliage. Before he entered the leaves the prince looked back briefly at his brothers who seemed to have begun an official tour of this arboreal castle. After following a mazy route Witherwing emerged behind his guide into a leafless space through which spread the limbs of a vast dead tree, white and without bark, a cage of bone in a sea of green. A large cluster of sticks was lodged in the cleft of two white branches, on the upward slope of one of which had been carved a set of steps.

"This is where the old one lives," said his guide. "You may go to him."

Witherwing passed by the Forester and mounted the white steps to what looked like an enormous rook's nest, though he knew it would contain a chamber like the one in which he had spent the night. Having ducked through the entrance he stopped and looked unseeingly into the unlit interior. There was neither movement nor sound as Witherwing's eyes gradually became accustomed to the gloom, and the weak light that filtered through the entrance and through small cracks in the walls of stick revealed nothing apart from those sticks. No other entrance was visible and no one had followed the prince up the steps to this seemingly empty room; perhaps this was a test, or a trick. Witherwing remained where he stood, his eyes fixed upon darkness. And then at last something flickered in that darkness and the prince found himself looking into two disembodied eyes.

"Welcome, winged one," creaked a disembodied voice.

For a moment Witherwing felt that he was facing an enchantment fit for a bard's tale, but he soon realized that a Forester's body would be virtually indistinguishable from a background like this and throughout the ensuing interview he made out no more of the old one's body than those eyes which he had seen first. He returned the greeting and the old one began again.

"I have waited for you a long time, but that is no trial for one who lives with trees. It seemed to me that they had forgotten you, and perhaps they had for a while. But you have seen this Hess and he would not have left his cave or tomb or castle or whatever his dwelling is in the Upper Lands without some purpose. It is possible that this purpose may involve the saving of Tum-Barlum, but his ends are his own. Some play is about to begin or be continued. And you, winged one, are to be a player. I knew your father and I knew his second queen. I am not to blame."

There followed a long silence in which something prevented Witherwing from questioning or commenting. He felt instinctively that his strength might lie in some form of detachment—not indifference or aversion to action, but in trying to hold steadily on to himself in a world of half-revelations and unaccountable powers.

"You have heard of Kryll?" the voice went on.

"Yes, I have heard of Kryll and his lake," said Witherwing. "He is said to work wonders."

"He is. It is Kryll you must seek out first in pursuit of the part you are to play. He is used to white birds coming to him from us. In terms of Tum-Barlum, its kings, princes and bards you are given a hero's part. You need see no more than that, though Kryll may have his own truths to tell. There are horns casting long shadows over you and your people and it is given to you to find them. Hrasp is a formidable enemy who carries death on his head; your's may be there. There is little point in looking beyond them. It was said long ago that horn and wing should meet and struggle, but I thought it had been forgotten."

Silence again. The old one closed his eyes and disappeared entirely.

"Am I to learn more here?" asked Witherwing. "I have travelled far for this."

"And you have much further to go, yet you may not learn much more. Perhaps you should not want to, for you have been given a hero's quest and if you do your part you may save your people and win power for your red-bearded brother. If you are wanting to find yourself, then that is not the quest with which I am concerned now. You may have heard that there are masters and makers, but first here is Kryll and then Hrasp—and these will take you far from the horizons of Tum-Barlum. That is enough. I am glad to have seen the winged one."

The eyes had not reappeared and the silence was not broken by the old one again. Witherwing thanked the invisible Forester and retired. The brightness outside took him by surprise and the bleached branches which held the dwelling of the old one were a pain to his sight. He was led back to where he had witnessed the dance of the Forest Folk on the previous day and there he was left alone until his companions returned. Harand was not among them. He had been conducted, Brandyll said, to the old one. No more performances were mounted by the Forest Folk—indeed, very few of them were in evidence—and the warriors of Tum-Barlum found that time was heavy on their hands. They had tired of the plentiful but tasteless food and drink provided for them and after they had exchanged a few remarks about the tree-world which they had been exploring, commenting on the surprising extent of the chambers carved inside the tree-trunks and on the infathomable complexity of routes, levels, bridges and passages, they fell into a drowsy silence in which, lulled by the whisper of a sea of leaves, they sensed again the rhythmic sway of the giant trees.

When Harand returned his face was blotched with angry red.

"We're leaving!" he blustered. "Let's start to pack up now and be on our way. Let's get back down to earth again. We'll head out along the edge of the Swamplands and come into Tum-Barlum that way."

Preparations began immediately. Harand paid scant attention to anyone, but it was particularly noticeable that he avoided looking at Witherwing. Brandyll attempted to question him, but he would not be drawn out until his troop had been guided down to the deep forest floor and was mounted again. A single Forester remained with them to take them to where the woods bordered on the Swamplands and Harand, still evidently gripped by his fury, refused to acknowledge the presence of his brown, spidery guide. Brandyll tackled his eldest brother again as they rode and he had said no more than a couple of words before Harand's rage and frustration came spilling out; his neck and brow were lividly knotted while his body twitched convulsively.

"Damn them! Damn them! I ought to take an axe to them and chop the woody bastards down for firewood. I ought to burn the bastards up and dance round the flames and roast some stinking Snakeskins over them or any other damn mutants I can round up in this disgusting forest. And I expect the place is full of them. It's like an open sore, this pox-ridden forest. It's running with filth like these stick-things. I'd like to cut it out. They have the audacity to take me to this 'old one' as if I were to deal with a man and when I get to this damn bird's nest there's nobody there at all. *Nobody!* Just this kind of creaking again, as if I were supposed to understand that. I kicked those damn sticks about a bit, I can tell you."

Brandyll waited, in case there were more curses to come, then said:

"Did you understand nothing?"

"What do you mean?" Harand snapped back pugnaciously, sensing criticism.

"Of this creaking, I mean. Were there words?"

"Well, there were some. But they were damn-fool words to have come all this way for. These twigs might just as well have got little brother here to fly to them with his little white wing, since this seems to be his business not ours."

Brandyll let the subject drop at this point and it was not resumed till the next day's journey when the trees began to shrink to a more familiar scale as the troop neared the Swamplands. He elicited from a somewhat calmed brother that there was, after all, something for Harand in this dark affair initiated by Hess—and stretching into the past who knew how far. But it seemed that there were to be no heroics for Harand, only the possibility of acquiring the kind of power that had scorched Tum-Barlum with the arrival of the Queen of Dread. Harand tried strenuously to ingratiate himself with Witherwing.

"No," he said, "the questing and heroics are not for me. Not for old Harand. He's got to stay around and wait to be King. They want the littlest brother for this one, and I'm not surprised. I've always said I wanted you on my side and by my side, little brother, and I remember how you stood up against the Horde when you were no more than a boy and if anyone can steal this fire from the Upper Lands it's you. I know it is. I have faith in you. Even if it comes to dealing with that horned bastard Hrasp. Though how one little brother with a wing can be expected to take on such a bull of a man who commands a whole army I don't . . . . But I have faith in you, remember that. And remember that there's a special place for you in Tum-Barlum's High Hall when I am king. And for Brandyll here, of course. . . ."

Here the Forester who had been guiding the troop turned to Harand, probably to indicate that he had brought them close to the Swamplands and that they would be able to find their own way from here. He reached a knotted, spidery arm toward Harand's cloak and the Prince, who had been facing his brothers and giving them his full attention, spun round in alarm, drawing his sword as he did so. Without pause he slammed the blade into the skull of the Forester, revealing to his appalled brothers that, whatever the exterior semblance of these Forest Folk, their blood and brains were like that of any other man. As the brown body toppled to the ground something stirred beneath the inscrutable arrangement of black rags which adorned it and a white bird fluttered into the air and disappeared in the leaves overhead.

All the warriors watched it go and then began to eye the surrounding trees uneasily, remembering the virtual invisibility of the Forest Folk against the background of the woods.

"Uergh!" exclaimed Harand, shaking the gore from his weapon. "It's no more than a bunch of firewood. Let's have no fuss about that. I'm damned if I'm going to be attacked by a bundle of sticks. Anyway we're almost out of the woods now and they'll never follow us beyond. Let's move on now. I want to get some hunting done soon. Some real hunting."

And that is what he did when, after a further

day's travel, they reached the line where forest and Swamplands began to merge. He took with him two old and experienced warriors and disappeared into the marshes with spears and nets, having told his brothers that he would be gone for about three days and that the rest of the troop might do as they pleased under their supervision. Most chose to fish quietly or to make unhurried sorties back into the woods to hunt for treerats or pigrats, while some simply maintained the camp. Witherwing spent some time in conversation with Brandyll concerning what had taken place among the Forest Folk and then he felt the need to be alone, to sort out his impressions, to dwell upon his uncertainties and to prepare himself for a prolonged and taxing absence from his home in search of . . . what? Of conflict, certainly, of old wonder-workers, and of a dubious means to power coveted by his eldest brother.

Witherwing rode away after a morning of talk with Brandyll till he came to a stream that threw itself in white arcs from slabs of black rock as it descended through the trees to the marshy lands beyond. By a deep pool at the base of one of these falls he tethered his horse, stripped and then bathed himself. He had caught three fishes and was roasting them over a small fire when he suddenly became aware that he was being observed from the opposite bank. Raising his eyes he expected to see the spidery forms of some of the Forest Folk, but instead he was confronted by the uncanny beauty of two children with pale green-tinged skin, wide straight mouths and hair almost the color of fresh blood.

"Why do you have a bird's wing?" said the boy.

"Well, I once wanted to fly," Witherwing answered.

"Can you?"

"No. Well, maybe *half* fly. And why do you have a snake's skin."

"It's not a snake's. It's ours," said the girl.

"Do you eat fish?" the prince asked.

"Well, yes we do," said the boy, "but we don't have any just now. I'm sure we'd give you some if we did. Do *you* like fish?"

"Yes. That's why I'm cooking these. But, you see, I have three fish and there's only one of me and so I was rather hoping I might find two other people to eat the others."

Witherwing adjusted his catch over the flames to ensure it was cooked evenly.

"I don't suppose you'd care to help me eat these?" he asked.

"Well, do you kill people?" the boy wanted to know.

"Oh no. Not unless they're very bad and try to kill me first."

"Then I think we would like to help you eat your fish," said the boy.

"And we promise we won't kill you," said the girl.

With that they dived like otters into the water and emerged a few moments later, their red hair glistening and plastered to their heads and shoulders, on the rock where Witherwing sat. They sat with him by the fire.

"Can we feel your wing?" asked the boy.

Witherwing assented and fanned it out.

"It's nice," said the girl. "I should like to have one."

"It *is* nice," Witherwing agreed, "but it's difficult to hold things with it."

"Can you hold fish with it?" the boy inquired,

gazing up into the trees as if food were far from his thoughts.

"Let's see, shall we?" said the prince as he handed out the fish.

They ate fast and in silence.

"You did manage to hold it," observed the boy when he had finished. "But not with your wing."

"I liked the fish," said the girl. "I'm surprised that you couldn't have eaten all of them. I think I could have. Look, there's my mother."

Witherwing looked to the opposite bank where the girl pointed and saw three women with the same greenish skin and blood-red hair as the children with whom he had dined. He did not know how long they had been observing him, but they were taut and suspicious.

"It's all right," called the boy. "He doesn't kill people."

"And his wing's nice," the girl added.

One of the women dived into the stream with the same grace that the children had shown. When she was safely ashore the second dived and the process was repeated with the third. They showed the same care in the way they disposed themselves on the rock, fanning out so that the prince could not see all three at once. He himself was still naked after his swim and his sword lay with his clothes behind him. These women were not to be trifled with, he could tell.

"I thank you for your children's company," he said. "We have passed a pleasant meal together."

Witherwing hoped that the Snake skins adhered to the Tum-Barlum convention that the sharing of food conferred mutual obligation; it was one of the few ways in which a traveller could find protection. He told his name, his origin and something of the

65

journey which he was now making; again he was following the rules of Tum-Barlum and he hoped that they would apply here. It seemed that they did for the eldest of the three women, the mother of the children, invited the prince to their encampment. Witherwing had been about to refuse politely when his eyes fastened upon one of the younger women and, moved by her strange beauty, he was choked with desire. Her own green eyes gave back his feeling and his stay with the Snakeskins became in that moment a short and burning involvement with that one girl. They kept apart from her people for the most part, and this appeared to be acceptable. Her love had come to him like an unexpected flame licking from the depths of her hereditary isolation, rolling a while round the dark walls of his. He would have liked to have taken her with him to his father's hall, though he knew that Harand's violent feelings about what he called "mutants" were not uncommon in Tum-Barlum, and anyway, she had been willing to stay with him for only two nights in the woods before slipping away, leaving him to fancy her green eyes in the leaves of many a spring tree.

When he had returned to his companions Witherwing found Harand back from his hunting and in high spirits. The young prince could not rid himself of the impression that there was something sinister in the way his brother had sated himself with killing; it was as if he had been drinking blood. Witherwing wondered what kind of creatures Harand had pursued; it was never mentioned.

But now, after Hess and the old one of the Forest Folk, Witherwing had his own hunting to do in lands less familiar than even the deep forest. He had been a man apart on his return to Tum-Barlum and, though the bard had prophezied a heroic fulfilment for his coming journey and Harand had struggled to keep up a flow of bluff encouragement, the reaction of Rumi and his court to Witherwing caused him to feel as if he were marked by death, as if he had already crossed some dividing line.

Another line was crossed when the solitary horseman rode down into the Flatlands at nightfall in the waning of the year.

4

"I am Prince Witherwing."

The rider had paused at the fringe of an earth-tent encampment of the Flatland folk. He spoke in answer to a challenge delivered by a youth with a stave, and at his announcement brown faces of women and children peered out from shadowy earth-doors while men fell back, making a passage for Witherwing to the fire. Respectfully the prince dismounted and walked toward the seated patriarch, who welcomed him.

"The bards have sung of you and your sister has married into the Flatland folk. Let there be no mine or thine between us."

Witherwing answered in the dignified formula expected of him.

"Long may you be a river to your people. I serve you."

"Rest and eat."

The small band of Flatland folk gathered around the fire and food was brought—hot broths of fibrous roots and rabbit meat, thickened with goat curd. Great lean dogs in hope of bones prowled round the edges of the group or sprawled close to the flames, their long noses flat on out-stretched paws.

A bowl of heavy bark-liquor was brought to Witherwing by a girl whose brown body seemed sculpted by the winds of the plain, such was the delicacy of dark hollow at the cheek and eye. Like most Flatlanders she was richly freckled and a glow of deep ginger burned in her thick hair.

Witherwing kept his cloak down over his left side, though he sensed that all were fascinated by what he concealed. Not that such wonders were unprecedented, for some said they had heard of other winged or partly feathered men. The Flatlanders had themselves seen a wandering band of Yellowmanes whose hair grew from head, neck and shoulders, running down the middle of the back and forming a short tail at the base of the spine. In the swamp country, where some of them had retreated when the Horde overran the plains, they had had dealings with the retiring Snakeskins, and the complexion of a couple of their own band suggested a Snakeskin strain in their ancestry. Witherwing recalled the Snakeskin girl's weird beauty which had stirred him so deeply. In loving her he had crossed another of those lines which separated him from his brothers and he still wished that he could have passed even further from them in the pursuit, for this love had swept up out of silence and fallen so swiftly back into silence that it was hard to attach a meaning to it or, perhaps, to believe that it had really happened. He was haunted by a dream of running water, green trees, a green body and blood-red hair. There was a legend in Tum-Barlum of a young king of great promise who had renounced his throne to pursue just such a dream of a girl once glimpsed who had seemed to speak with the voice of his own soul. All she had spoken was his name. Witherwing found it all too easy to hear his name whispered when the wind blew through the leaves of the forest or the grasses of the Flatlands.

After food the patriarch raised his bowl to Witherwing, saying:

"May our ways be together."

Without appearing to be pressing, he was asking the traveller to explain his intentions. His first motive was self-protection, for travellers were often bearers of trouble even when not hostile to their hosts. But secondly, all the Flatlanders sensed the possibility of tales to match the bards."

"I am bound for the city of Karn-Ingli," said Witherwing. "But I serve you for your kindness. There came through Tum-Barlum one who spoke of the glowing stones of the Queen of Dread, and my way is now to Lizard Lake to seek out deep-minded Kryll who is said to work wonders. From there I shall go to the Upper Lands and the region of Hrasp."

There was uneasy movement among his listeners at the mention of Hrasp. The patriarch considered, then spoke:

"The name of Hrasp-the-Hunter sounds ill to herdsmen of the plains. For when great cold comes, then Hrasp is driven down to plunder. And he is devoted to cruelty, and untouched by age. Though I am old my father was gored by Hrasp, and many that I knew died at the hands of the Karns. But I have heard it said that wing and horn shall meet and struggle."

So, thought Witherwing, my doom is known in the Flatlands. The horn of which the patriarch spoke referred to Hrasp-the-Hunter, who ruled Karn-Ingli in the Upper Lands where ice-peaks rode up high above the mountains of stone. Like the woolly snowbulls of that region Hrasp bore on his head great branching antlers which dealt out slaughter as profusely as his sword.

"Tell me," said Witherwing, "do those horns grow from him, or are they no more than my helmet's lizard-crest?"

"One who is winged is familiar with wonders," the old man replied. "I have known a man who said he tore them from Hrasp's head in battle; but his wits were something crazed, and now he's dead. There is much that we cannot know, but it is certain that death sits at those antler points."

The most repeated proverbs of all the peoples Withering had met stressed death as the only certainty. This was a world without much knowledge of the past beyond a few generations back, yet it seemed an old and dying world.

Witherwing was aware that he took a risk in openly declaring his purpose to his Flatland hosts, for somehow news seemed to outrun any traveller. And almost certainly some of Hrasp's men would now be moving secretly among the herdsmen of the plain, gathering information against the day when the bitter cold would bring them down to prey upon the Flatlands. Scattered bands of nomadic Flatlanders could offer little resistance to the fierce and disciplined Upland warriors, and wives, flocks and lives were uneasy possessions in a severe winter. Hrasp's men, in the distinctive fur of the white bear or the thick blue skin of the manfish, had never yet crossed into Tum-Barlum, but since the visit of Hess it was evident that this was only a matter of time. At least, Witherwing reasoned, this openness would suggest that he was moving against Hrasp-the-Hunter, which was likely to make friends of the Flatlanders.

Hess and the old one of the forest had suggested more questions than answers and this had been, perhaps, their intention. These Flatlanders had no interest in veiling truths from Witherwing, though he continued beset with uncertainties from what they now told him. They had heard rumors that the power of the glowing stones had manifested itself in the Upper Lands, though quite how they did not know; also they were unable to say whether or not Hrasp and his people controlled that power, or were controlled by it. There had been talk too of a white-faced woman with thin red lips who had been seen at Hrasp's ice-caves in past years. Witherwing feared that he was in pursuit of his nightmare.

The Queen of Dread had disappeared as soon as Rumi's sons had been restored to him; that she had left no trace of where she went was ascribed to witchcraft, and it had been judged useless to search for her. She left behind her one small glowing stone which burned and wasted the attendant who kept it, and Rumi had ordered that it be taken to the world's end and thrown into the sea. Its keeper journeyed on foot to the sea, threw the stone from a high cliff, and then jumped himself into the gray smoking waves.

It was too obscure to be called a memory, but the impression had always remained with Witherwing that he and his brothers had been delivered back to Tum-Barlum *by the Queen*. It was not far removed from his nightmare of ascent, for he seemed to fall out of the skies, his brothers asleep around him. And the earth of his home rushed up toward him. A white face. Thin red lips. Glittering eyes.

This was not how the bard told it.

More bark-liquor was brought. It made Witherwing feel heavy as earth, not dull, but comfortable and, for a time, as if he belonged.

"Since you go to the Upper Lands," said the patriarch, "I have a gift for you."

He made a motion with his walnut-brown hand, and the girl who had brought drink to Witherwing stepped forward guiding a pale and blank-faced child. He appeared an idiot.

"Hutt the brother of Nada will go with you," said the old man to Witherwing, who frowned, seemed about to speak, but decided upon silence and waiting.

The patriarch nodded.

"You are wise. Hutt is white and he has no tongue. But he sees where eyes and words do not reach. It is a godlike knowledge and sees into men's minds. It is dangerous, but you will need it to fight dangers."

Witherwing had heard of such white children with all-seeing minds, whose heightened mental sense seemed to have used up many other human faculties. Skin and hair were drained of color; they were dumb; and they never grew up. Witherwing knew that this band of Flatlanders would be unlikely to have more than one such child. This was their highest gift. He looked again into Hutt's eyes, seeing now that they were not empty, but deep as a mirror or pool. Throwing back his cloak he extended his white wing toward the child and brushed his pale face with soft feathers.

"Hutt."

The child did not move, but the depths of his eyes seemed to give back all that was in Witherwing's mind. It was misty and troubled.

The wing, withdrawing, touched lightly on the breast of the boy's sister.

Witherwing thanked the patriarch in such a way that he showed he knew the value of the gift.

Out of courtesy he entertained his hosts with his own story—the official version, not his visionary uncertainties. Firelight threw a rich sheen upon the brown or brindled faces of his hearers. Children slept at their mothers' breasts, while those a little older struggled against drowsiness so as to miss none of the wonder told by the man with the wing. The group appeared like a raft on a vast and placid dark sea over which swung the constellations, clear and cold. Old men related mysterious half-tales which had no beginnings or endings; neither did they have easily recognized meanings, though they glowed, as it were, with a hazy intensity as if meaning surrounded them. They conjured up images of gods who had once walked the earth, who had made sea and sky their own, and from whose fingers ran fiery rivers that had burned the world.

There were long silences beneath the stars, and a barely perceptible pallor smudged the horizon before the Flatlanders retired to their earthtents. Witherwing chose to sleep beneath a herdsman's canopy set under a solitary bent tree a little apart from the encampment. Squatting by the fire Hutt stared into the flames and made no preparation for rest. Gradually silence fell, broken occasionally by movements among the sheep or tethered goats. Witherwing wrapped wing and cloak closely around him and drifted toward sleep.

He woke with an internal start almost immediately, it seemed, after falling asleep. With no apparent movement his fist closed upon the bone handle of his knife, and slowly he raised his eyelids to see, as he had sensed, a black shape standing over him. In complete stillness Witherwing gathered all his energies to a point ready to spring with all the speed of a snake's neck.

A pause.

Then, instead of a leap and flash of blade, Witherwing's cloak opened slowly. He half-raised himself upon his arm, stood, and looked into the dark hollows of Nada's eyes. She raised her arms to his neck; they were thin, strong, and delicately freckled. Witherwing thought of wind and earth. Her blanket fell to the ground and her naked skin tensed against the night cold. With a rustling sigh a great swan's wing enveloped her back, and the blood of the pair beat like a bird's flight. His mouth moved over her like the wind. Her love was rich wine, strong and spreading as the plain which was her home.

She spoke a little of that home to Witherwing, and he tried to convey to her something of the underside of his thoughts, his unexplained dream images.

"Hutt will help you," she said. "For he will see them too. But you must learn his language, for he won't speak ours. He means us to go inside, quietly. I don't think I shall see him again, for the white children have short lives. If I say 'Be good to him,' it is for your sake; he has more knowledge and power than we do. Perhaps you will come back."

She was gone. Like the Snakeskin woman.

Witherwing lay deep within a cave of green ice, unconscious at first of the distant white light. But soon it shone insistently through the thick ice walls, calling to him. And at length he responded and came to the iron green surface which enclosed him. He began to pass through the glassy cold, which became progressively lighter until he burst into the white glare outside.

He awoke in the wolf-light to find Hutt squatting a few paces from his head, staring at him. So this was how the boy spoke. Hutt turned his head and looked into the middle distance. Witherwing knew it was for his benefit and, though Hutt's manner seemed so blank, he knew too that this was important. Therefore he was mystified to find himself peering long and hard in the gray light at an undramatic flock of sheep. An animal would move and perhaps bleat from time to time, but that was all . . .

And then he saw that what he had taken for a sheep was no such thing. At the far side of the flock a man clothed in white fur slipped silently away into the morning mist. Witherwing saw the light flash of his face as he turned round before disappearing. Had the intruder at that moment sensed the eyes upon him? Or, perhaps, the mind?

5

Winds bent the grasses of the Flatlands throughout
Witherwing's journey with Hutt. The boy rode beside him on a long-haired pony, whose mane
streamed like the cloaks of the riders. There were
occasional swamps and low scrub-woods, but travel
was not generally difficult. Sometimes they were
able to use the wide green ridgeways that mysteri-
ously crossed the Flatlands in great sweeping curves
and straight level stretches impossible for the paths
made by men. They saw piles of unfamiliar stones
that had the look of broken columns, suggesting,
had not the scale and purpose been inconceivable,
the remains of gigantic bridges. For food Witherwing trapped rabbits at the end of a day's travelling,
and Hutt's all-seeing sense had saved him from setting nooses at the burrows of the obscenely fat and
hairless breed which survived, probably, only because their flesh was inedible to men and foxes alike.
Encampments of Flatland bands, like Hutt's, received and fed them, asked for news and tales, and
stored the visit of the winged prince and the white
child as a wonder to be turned out and contemplated like a precious object in the nights to come
around their fires.

77

As he moved nearer to the Upper Lands Witherwing sensed increasing fear among the Flatlanders he encountered; the winds were promising a hard winter and most bands had stories of sighting small numbers of Hrasp's men. The herdsmen led harsh lives, pressed between marauders and uncertain weather. Yet they endured with some dignity, and Witherwing hoped that he might serve them. He would not know until he had consulted Kryll at the Lizard Lake in the mountains.

To be with Hutt was outwardly calm, but inwardly disquieting for Witherwing. The boy's silent presence seemed to force a relentless introspection in him, causing him to question all the standards of his people and himself, the purpose of his present journey, and the truth of the bardic version of his own story. What were his dreams, that they sometimes seemed more real than his passage over this shadowy plain? The Snakeskin woman and Hutt's dark sister had slipped unchecked from him, like other less well-remembered girls—had he sent them away? Was he ungenerous, and was there a better way to know them than through his mournful feeling for beauty and delicate strength? Could there be more than a sweet exchange of sadnesses in the dark? When he had first heard of the white children with their special powers of mind Witherwing had assumed that they would bring forth answers; but uncomfortable questions swam up to him from the depths of Hutt's eyes.

A strong yet curious bond was formed between Witherwing and the white boy. In that their minds when desired, were open to each other and their communication wordless and complete the relationship was closer than anything the prince had ex-

78

perienced. At the same time it was less than other relationships, for where Witherwing had normally grown to know others by gradual familiarity with the jaggedness of their idiosyncracies, with Hutt no such exploration was possible. He was like a window; he worked by vacancy, by being seen through. For Witherwing, to be with Hutt was like being with a ghost of some part of himself. When he looked into Hutt's mind it was as if his scrutiny were turned inward and, often, when Hutt broke into his thoughts it did not seem like an intrusion, but as if something surfaced in a secret lake that the prince bore within him. So in some ways Hutt was as much a mirror as a window to Witherwing, though, because of the descent that was necessary to look into it, familiar or reassuring images were not generally given back. Witherwing began to recognize that in learning to cope with Hutt's unsettling powers he was learning to live with himself, seeking another way toward knowledge of what that self might be. His use of the boy's mind was sparing, partly because it opened trapdoors that might have no steps beneath them and partly because a difficult, sometimes impossible task of interpretation was thrust upon him by the images he received. Visions of a reality stranger than any bardic tale could stream from the pale, silent boy. His power seemed to the prince richer than anything that might be gained from the half-legendary glowing stones of the Upper Lands, but the possibility of nightmare lay within it too; whether the nightmare began in Hutt, or in Witherwing himself, or in the world around them the prince could not know.

On one occasion Witherwing silently communicated to Hutt the half-song of the Forest Folk, that he might even have dreamed he heard:

> There's makers and masters
> > And Time upon Time.
> Theres change and diasters
> > And Time and more Time.
>
> There's masters and players
> > And Time and the Game.
> Theres no place for prayers
> > To the Masters of Game.

In response there flowed from Hutt an inscrutable dream that was marked by both sharpness and fluidity. The dominating image was a godlike figure in deep, reverential meditation before a flat surface on which differently colored and shaped carvings were arranged. The figure seemed intent upon moving one or more of these pieces; yet it was clear that worlds of thought must be passed through before any such move could be made. Witherwing sensed that there were rules, conventions and symbols governing the projected move that were beyond him, as if the other-worldly thinker was about to rearrange sun, moon and stars. While the unaging figure remained still, the landscape which lay about him changed as though ages passed and cataclysms were reduced to a passing whisper in an eternity of contemplation. The landscape began watery, developed into solid green, faded to brown and returned to green, was consumed by fire, blackened, then covered by shining crystal constructions over which lightnings played; then darkness and heaps of broken images, red rocks and dust, winds which filled the air with the dust in which dark shapes began to move, falling towers and something swarming, more fire. And as these cycles continued the central figure of the vision began at last to stir. He seemed almost ready to touch the pieces on the board before him, but while he raised his hands the board itself began to reform and the carved pieces, translucent-like glass, disposed themselves in intricate arrangements in the air as a flat surface became a cubic space. The thinker, his hands suspended, continued to meditate on the game, still abstracted and god-like. Then one of the pieces, a globe of clear glass at first, grew flecked with red and an indefinable form developed within it. Other globes began to show a similar process and the thinker smiled and put his hand to one, shifted it and smiled again when he saw a further change of shape which triggered changes in neighboring globes—for all the pieces were globes now. The fine white hands created a dazzling dance among them—patterns, colors and forms shifted and twined like music while from the arid plain behind the player came the faint sound of wind.

The player's manipulations of his glass pieces grew feverish and it seemed to Witherwing that the new forms he was creating within the beads were growing monstrous and somehow their juggling was rearranging the landscape. There was an atmosphere of clinical violence now and the player came to resemble Hess at the bloody sports that Harand had arranged. Witherwing's body ached; his wing pained him. He felt as if he were being hatched in one of those glass beads and had a momentary vision as from the inside of one of them of a huge white face grinning at him, thin-lipped, sharp-eyed.

The sound of wind increased and a cloud of dust blew up around the player who pulled a hood about his face and fell asleep, the glass game suspended before him. So the giant figure was still and seemed set to remain so, while on the plain there were periodic tiny movments from things that hopped and wriggled, insects with horns or wings.

The scouring wind spoke with the voice of the Forest Folk:

> There's death and forgetting
>   And ends, but no end.
> And still there is fretting
>   After the end.
>
> There's masters and makers
>   There's horn and there's wing
> There's blood and there's battle
>   For poets to sing.

And so the vision ended.

In practical matters Hutt proved unexpectedly useful for one who was incapable of much action. Certainly he was far from the liability that Witherwing had feared. Apart from his help in trapping, he would signal the prince to edible root vegetables, and the boy was infallible in seeking out water. Witherwing had no need even to mention that it was time to replenish their waterskins; Hutt knew what passed in his mind. Nor was it necessary to keep watch at night, for Hutt rarely rested, and when he did his mind still encompassed all that went on around him. Once Witherwing had risen from sleep, tethered his horse which had broken loose, and lain down again before he realized that he had been summoned by the sleeping Hutt to do this.

After twelve days the mountains of the Upper Lands showed on the horizon like a blue smoke, and three more brought Witherwing and Hutt to the foothills which rose with dramatic suddenness from the plain. The herbage was rich here, but the Flat-landers had deserted it at the approach of winter. No one wanted to be first in line for Hrasp-the-Hunter.

While Witherwing was on the plain, the maps which he had brought from Tum-Barlum, crudely inked on fat-rabbit skin, had been generally useless except where they indicated green ridgeways. Now he was able to take his bearings by some minor peaks and Manfish Mountain, so called for the long pla-teau which made it appear a gigantic half-animate sea-beast stretched out among the hills. They en-tered the hill country where a harsh-sounding river, white and troubled, spilled out from the Upper Lands. Witherwing looked upon the black rocks against which the torrent hissed and foamed, and he felt, as when Hutt's eyes were on him, that he was seeing into the confusion of his own mind. This was the stream he was to follow to its source, and as he travelled up it, the violence of its descent steadied into a drone almost reassuring to the prince. He perceived a stark and invigorating beau-ty in the black and white collision of rock and water, so that it seemed not chaos but only momen-tum like that of the hot blood in his own body or the distant wheeling of the stars.

Hutt could pluck silver fish from the river with an ease that amazed Witherwing, who never saw any life beneath the surface. They roasted these sweet-tasting fish at evening, drank water from the river, and slept wrapped in their cloaks beneath a dwarfish mountain tree. None of Witherwing's brothers, nor anyone at Rumi's hall save the king himself, had made the journey to these mountains. Rumi had followed the same river when he had sought out deep-minded Kryll whose help he needed when the Queen of Dread had deprived him of his children. The king had never spoken of what he had learned from Kryll, and, more strange, the bards offered no account of what passed at their meeting when the family tale was told in verse.

Next morning a chill mist from the river dampened Witherwing's spirits almost as much as his clothes. He did not attempt to light a fire, and he chewed upon some unpalatable cold fish left from the previous night. Hutt appeared unmoved by physical discomfort, and mentally neutral as ever. In their habitual silence they saddled their horses and moved slowly upstream. By midday the mist still had not cleared and their progress seemed even slower than it actually was.

As they were about to enter a defile that loomed obscure and gray before them, Witherwing was struck violently on the forehead. He jerked to a stop, stunned and baffled. There had been nothing which could have delivered the blow, and when his head was clear of the searing yellow flash he felt no pain, there was no blood, and still no sign of what had hit him. Spinning around toward the boy, he knew at once what had happened; his mind crowded with images of danger. Hutt had stopped him from entering the gorge and was now signalling, with great mental vividness and urgency, that there was a source of danger up on the left-hand rock face. A secondary danger spot was also indicated at the far end of the defile, but that would have to wait. Witherwing waved Hutt off his pony and indicated that he should follow. Slapping the horses, he sent them clattering between the steep rocky sides, and himself swung off in a wide arc to the left. His movements were swift and deliberate, for he was able to sense where the danger lay as if a great light was shining before him and he was closing relentlessly upon it. Somehow he also knew the degree of this hazard; he was outnumbered, but surprise would be on his side. When it occurred to him that he was unaware of the nature of his enemy —was it man, furbeast, or something even more formidable?—he remained unshaken. Hutt would tell him all he needed to know.

What his swan's wing lacked as an aid to gripping was more than compensated by its balancing function for Witherwing. Subtle flaps and sweeps enabled him to leap nimbly from rock to rock as could no ordinary man. Soon he had reached the top of the gorge, more than three times the height of Rumi's lizard-capped High Hall. Below him the river, invisible under thick layers of curling mist, clashed loud between its rock walls; he would not have to worry unduly about making a soundless approach. Unclasping his cloak, he let it rest damply among the rocks so that he could move freely. His lizard-skin tunic would provide a good measure of protection. He ruffled the feathers at his left side and shook his freed wing. There was a scraping hiss and on his right side a white blade sliced experimentally at the mist. Crouching slightly Witherwing advanced, his sword like a sensitive antenna before him.

After a few minutes Witherwing slid like a gray ghost behind a large boulder, then peered intently down to the rim of the gorge not far below him. Dimly outlined in the mist were four figures grouped around a high pile of stones from which protruded a thick wooden lever. Through the sensitivity granted to him by Hutt the prince could feel the anxiety of the men, and he fed greedily upon it. The four had not counted upon the fog in their plans. Now they were straining to judge the location of the horses below from the hoofbeats which rose to them, but the narrowness of the gorge and the boiling of the river tumbled all sounds together confusingly. Two men, their shapes large and fuzzy on account of the furs they wore, leaned over the edge while the other two gripped the lever in the rockpile, ready to send their lethal avalanche spinning down upon the horses. Witherwing could see that, had he been riding below, there would have been little chance of escape, for even if he, Hutt, or their horses had not been directly hit by rocks, the fall would have alarmed the horses enough to tip them from their narrow and slippery ledge to the ground between rock and water. Laying down his sword and selecting a large round pebble, Witherwing decided to save the horses if possible. Just as one of the figures bending out over the lip of the gorge raised his arm as a preliminary signal, Witherwing hurled the stone, striking him viciously in the small of the back. With an echoing howl of outrage the fur-clad warrior pitched over and disappeared down the foggy cleft.

Instantly the three remaining men whirled around, swords or bone-tipped spears at the ready. Above them towered a gray form with one vast wing outspread. As he jumped, Witherwing felt the bruising impact of a manfish-bone point when a spear glanced off his lizard-skin armor, and before the thrower had recovered his balance Witherwing's boot smashed into his shoulder and sent him reeling over the edge of the cliff. Sweeping hard down with his wing, which sent the mist eddying in whorls around him, the prince turned to face the other two. One was in fur, the other in the thick blue skin of the manfish; the prince would have to be quick and wary with his swordthrusts to penetrate that. Both rushed him at once. He momentarily blinded the one on his left by thrusting his wing into his face, at the same time blocking with his sword a savage downward slash of the other's blade. His arm was numbed by the ringing blow, but he was able to slip between the two so that he no longer had his back to the cliff edge. The furred warrior, light-skinned with cold milky eyes, eased toward him, then lunged at his chest. Witherwing parried with another swift downward stroke, and was about to make a return when he felt a stinging shock at his left shoulder where feather met flesh. A bright red stain spread among the snowy feathers; he stumbled backward and fell. A blade of razor-sharp bone had been thrown by the other Karn warrior, who watched impassively as his companion stood over the prince to hack his throat.

Before this could be done Witherwing raised and flapped his wing in the face of his assailant, and, in the instant that he thus gained, jabbed upward with his sword which entered between chin and neck and burst on up into the skull. Hrasp's warrior was biting on death; blood poured around his bared teeth, and his slanting eyes stared in mute surprise as he crashed down like a felled tree. There was no time to extricate his sword from the dead man's head, so Witherwing plucked the red-tipped bone knife from his shoulder and rolled away as the warrior in manfish-skin ran at him. Witherwing blocked one heavy swing of the other's sword, but it was clear that the knife would not stand many blows like that. As he raised his wing his opponent saw what was coming; or thought he did. For the warrior from the Upper Lands lunged forward and to Witherwing's right in order to avoid having the swan feathers rubbed in his face; he had seen that trick twice now. But Witherwing, instead of attempting to touch the Karn, beat his wing with great force twice, allowing him to shoot his body to the left, at the same time twisting round behind the forward-moving warrior to the back of whose neck he delivered a staggering blow. The Karn lurched away in precipitate retreat, almost falling upon Hutt, who at that moment appeared. The sword of Hrasp's man was quickly poised to slit the boy's skull and Witherwing could not act quickly enough to save him. He cried out in frustration.

But the brains of the frail white boy had not spilled. Instead the warrior was thrown back, his face torn by terrible strain as if the inside of his head had exploded. When the body fell to the ground it was rigid as if frozen. Hutt had not moved. Witherwing hoped he would never have such a child for an enemy.

Voices in the dialect of the Upper Lands drifted up the misty gorge, and Witherwing, the heat of battle still on him, bent his weight on the lever in the high-piled stones, releasing the deathly load. Almost immediately he regretted this as an unworthy action. Within himself he questioned even the worthiness of the battle he had just fought. By all the standards of Tum-Barlum his conduct had been faultlessly heroic; but, although he had always prevented himself from dwelling consciously upon this, he knew that there was often a grotesque disparity between the heroism celebrated by the bards and that which he witnessed in life. He had seen his eldest brother in skirmishes with the forest people killing from behind, slaughtering the unarmed and the wounded, and had later heard those deeds extolled in song as the flower of chivalry. Wither-wing's engagement with the Karn warriors was certainly not cowardly; but would he have done better simply to have avoided them? Like most of their people they were cruel and simple warriors. Was it right that he should meet them on their own terms? He had no answers. It was difficult to conceive of life other than in terms of struggle in this weary world. Perhaps Kryll would give guidance. Or Hutt. Witherwing gazed into the boy's eyes and saw only his own darkness and terror. Hutt had power, not morality; he would neither confirm nor deny a meaning in life.

Witherwing recovered his sword and Hutt handed him his green cloak. They continued along the top of the gorge until they could descend. There was no sign of their own horses, but they discovered the tethered mounts of six Karns, their manfish-skin saddles trimmed with white fur. Two of these they took, scattering the rest.

All that day the mists hung heavy round Witherwing.

6

Flushed with the sharp-tasting wine of Tum-Barlum,
Prince Harand, after meat in Rumi's High Hall,
turned to two of his younger brothers.

"Ring, Brandyll! Let us hunt tomorrow."

"Like today, like yesterday," answered Ring.
"I'm tired of chasing woodrats. I want to chase
women. So I won't come."

"I wasn't talking of woodrats. I know how you
can hunt *and* chase women. *I* know. I'm going to be
a king. I'm not just a killer of rats. I've killed more
men . . ."

"Yes, than your altogether too many years.
We know," said Ring. "What is your plan?"

Harand lowered his head and leeringly whispered:

"*Snakeskins.*"

"That is forbidden," said Brandyll.

"*Forbidden!* Are you not a man? Do you want
sport? Or do you want to catch mice in the corners
of your father's hall? Snakeskins are no more than
animals. We would do a service in hunting them
down. *I* have done it before."

"Then you should be ashamed," Brandyll

chided. "You have a brother who is winged, and yet you call the Snakeskins less than human."

"In so far as he has a wing he *is* less than human. Now among the rest of us, apart from a few oes and fingers more or less, there is nothing inhuman. We are not mutants. He is. If he does not return from the Upper Lands, we lose only that which disgraces our family. If he succeeds, then the glowing stones bring power to me . . . to our father . . . to us . . ."

"Much good they did us in the past," said Brandyll as he rose and moved away. "You are almost an old man, Harand. And you talk like a cruel and silly boy."

"Coward," muttered Harand in a sullen undertone.

"What was it like?" asked Ring.

"What?"

"Hunting Snakeskins."

Harand brightened.

"Oh *that!* There's nothing like it. It's like a woman after a fist. Woodrats, pigrats—whatever you like—they're never the same after Snakeskins. You can do it any way—nets, bows, spears."

7

The foothills rolled high away into distant blue.
Each ridge, when climbed, revealed another yet
higher to be tackled, and brooding over all, there was
the dark powerful shape of Manfish Mountain.
After the aching featurelessness of the great plain,
this country seemed like the body of a sleeping
giant strong and mysterious, in repose and yet not
motionless. Brown grasses and heather rippled with
the wide freedom of the sea and black rocks shouldered their way out of the earth. A light, sharp
and silver as steel, hovered over the landscape. Out
of the heart of the Upper Lands sliced a cold blast
alien as a seagull's eye. Witherwing's green cloak
lifted and clapped, and, in exhilaration without joy
so did his heart.

If this land was a giant then clearly he had
once woken or turned in his sleep, for, as with the
green ridgeways of the Flatlands, an air of ruin
emanated from the ground, a sense of unfamiliar
presences. There were more broken columns like
those of the plain, and great cracked blocks of gray
stone from which protruded tentacles of rusty metal. Once they came upon a huge and inexplicable
metal skeleton with the wind whistling through it

92

sunken ribs. Witherwing had heard of such things being found long ago in Tum-Barlum; his own sword may have been forged from one of them.

He paused with Hutt before the gaunt skeleton and tried to apprehend it through the boy's mind. Such communication through inner image and sensation was no longer strange to him, and he had begun to wonder if his own mind held the potential to see like Hutt's. Still the unjudging emotionless clarity of the boy's vision frightened him, for there was little enough to be certain of in the world as it was. Except death.

A wave from the white boy's mind flowed into Witherwing as he stood, outwardly abstracted, by the flaking cage, which soon began to glow with stupendous humming energy radiating wider and wider, spilling relentlessly to all points of the horizon, and on. And on. Fire running aglitter from the fingers of gods. Inhuman singing, knifelike and terrible. Bitter cold distance between stars which rang. Ice which flamed. Power; terror; destruction. A face white and flawless, baleful stars at its eyes, lips so thin, so red, so without feeling, they seemed fresh cut by the thinnest of all blades.

"Enough!" cried Witherwing within himself. He clutched his head, realizing that it was with his voice that he screamed too.

Was there no floor, no roof to this world? Might he just fall for ever? He dared not look into Hutt's deep eyes.

Manfish Mountain shimmered and faded in the silver light, and when Witherwing and Hutt breasted the next ridge, the brittle grass and heather gave place to rolling miles of black pinewood. The air swarmed with bright cold flecks which brushed their faces and melted, and which gave a crystalline

93

fleece to their cloaks. Snorting steam, the horses quivered the length of their bodies.

Hutt and Witherwing descended to a new and silent world. Thick black branches arched above them, and below them lay a muffling floor of immemorial pine needles. It was so dark that they hardly noticed when night fell. Through half the night a canopy of snow built up over the tops of the trees, with little reaching below except when a branch would sag beneath the weight of the white tent and scatter its soft load to the forest floor.

From time to time Witherwing used the boy's mind to keep his direction, though he was reluctant to feel that bleak all-seeing power. So it was with relief that he saw moonlight filter through the glowing snowy crust above, and where a break occurred he took his bearings by the stars in the cleared sky. At last a low and distant roar became audible, and Witherwing made toward it. It seemed they travelled through an endless palace with columns of black marble, heavy black drapes around them, black furs beneath them, and a roof of silvery alabaster. Toward dawn the canopy was flushed with pink, then suddenly, as the sun levelled its rays over Manfish Mountain, there were acres of crystallized blood above them, spreading a fiery luster through all the forest.

All the while the roaring sound grew louder.

The forest ended abruptly at a steep rocky scree. Removing their few provisions—strips of smoked woodrat and goatflesh, waterskins, weapons—from their mounts, the prince and the boy began the laborious climb up the mass of stones which continually shifted beneath them, sucking at their ankles. The horses had been abandoned, for Witherwing knew from his crude maps that an even greater climb awaited him.

For more than an hour their ears were filled with the grating of pebbles underfoot and the pounding of blood in their own heads, until they stood weary and silent at the top of the scree. And now the sound of falling water filled the air, for before them hung a long stripe of white mist of a height to terrify a Flatlander. From a table of rock, almost invisible far above, the waterfall leapt into empty air. It spread down in white folding veils, while from a shimmering forest of rainbow-arched spray at the base of the cliff rose an upward vaporous mirror-image of the waterfall. This contrary motion and the unprecedented height of the falls created an impression of dreamlike suspension. Witherwing, entranced, gazed long at the airy white pillar flanked by precipitous walls of blue snowdusted rock.

The prince dared to turn his mind to Hutt's, opening its door so that he might fully experience this awesome sight. But instead of the falls, the image of Hutt's sister, Nada, came to him, staring at him and moving closer. Quickly he closed himself to the boy's power; he did not want that image bleached of feeling. Still, it was a haunting picture. Nada had appeared conscious of being watched, and a sense of purpose had marked her approach.

The waters floated down and the mist rose.

For the rest of that day and night Witherwing and Hutt stayed close to a fire that had been built with difficulty, for they had not carried wood with them from the pine forest. But they were able to gather enough damp scrubby bushes to last them through the night. Witherwing trusted that the flames would deter the furbeast from troubling them, though he did not know if they were yet close enough to the Upper Lands to meet any of these creatures. Indeed, he knew very little about the furbeast—what it looked like, how, or even whether it would attack were mysteries to him. He had never heard a first-hand account of the confrontation with a furbeast, which was reputed to be among the greatest terrors of the Upper Lands.

As it were, the clear night passed without incident, and on the following cold blue day they began what seemed from a distance the impossible climb up the side of the falls. The steep path appeared to have been cut partly by a former course of the waterfall and partly by the titanic work of hands which had in places chiselled rough steps out of the granite. Sometimes their route took them through tunnels, and at others they passed behind the falls and climbed with the rushing sheets of spray at their backs. It was cold, wet, and wearying, but there were rewards, like the sight beneath them of the glittering roof of the pinewoods and the clear white receding peaks of the foothills through which they had travelled. As they neared the summit of the falls it appeared to Witherwing that the caves behind the water stretched deep into the cliff, and below the almost overpowering roar of waters he thought he detected the sound of slow animal movements from the granite depths.

Lizard Lake was metallic blue, almost black, with curling drifts of white vapor lifted from its surface by a wind which swept down the cold steeps of Manfish Mountain and slashed across the water giving even greater impetus to the racing swirl at the head of the falls. Glistening rocks of dark granite like ravaged teeth, projected from the waters, each rock being crowded with almost immobile lizards some the size of a man. As if involved in some impenetrable ritual all lay with their heads raised, their thin expressionless mouths clamped shut, their dark bright eyes alert and unsurpriseable. The scaled skin of the lizards, almost beyond price to Flatlanders, had undergone its annual transformation from green to white. Soon they would leave the water and take to the caves for the winter.

Like a charred finger, a black stone tower rose from the water. Its walls entirely covered the rock on which it had been built, so that it seemed to stand unsupported on the watery skin, or to have its foundations on the unreachable floor of Lizard Lake. An aggressively sharp conical roof topped the tower, the whole appearance of which suggested that it would sullenly jab at a sleeping god should one ever descend in his repose from the sky. White birds fluttered about the parapet.

There was no visible causeway leading out to the tower.

But when Hutt and Witherwing drew level with the tower along the bank the albino boy simply stepped into the dark steaming water and began to walk across its surface.

8

"Quiet. Keep low. But look," hissed Harand.

Ring, flat on his belly, softly parted the reeds before him and sucked in his breath excitedly. The sinuous bodies, green skin, and bright scarlet hair of the Snakeskin women caused in him a sexual palpitation which he unconsciously converted into blood-lust.

"Damn toads!" Ring whispered. "What do we do now?"

"We'll have a chase. They can run like hell, so we can work up a good sweat. I'll go back for the horses while you jump out and set them going. We'll give them a bit of a start, and then get after them with pigrat spears. I can't see any men, *er* males, so we shouldn't have to cope with weapons. They're cunning vermin, mind, but we've got nothing to worry about. Give me a minute, then get out and scare them off."

Harand slipped away through the reeds by the way they had come. After a short wait Ring, wrapped in the kind of thick green cloak that all the brothers wore, leapt into the swamp-clearing with his sword hewing the air before him. He bellowed incoherently, and five of the six Snakeskin women snatched up children and darted toward cover. But the sixth approached Ring, opening her arms as if in welcome; her breasts were pale green, with nipples like purple grapes.

"Witherw . . ." she began, but broke off seeing Ring's face.

He was puzzled and alarmed that she did not flee with the others, and he jabbed at her with his sword, at first just roughly prodding her; but when she still did not retreat he screamed and slammed the blade up to its hilt into her chest. She stumbled back, stared at him, and crimson, vivid as her hair, bubbled at her lips as she swayed sideways and fell softly as a swan.

There was no time for Ring to recover his sword before one of the other Snakeskin women had broken cover and, without cry or word, launched her body at him. For an instant he felt something like embarrassment, since he had not meant to start killing like this. He had wanted to hunt. How was he to rid himself of this lithe and slippery creature and force her to play the part of his quarry?

Such thoughts vanished as her teeth clamped like a wicked vice on his nose. Do what he would, Ring could not dislodge her, and soon he was waving his arms ineffectually as the pain and panic rose to the horrible accompaniment of crunching and gurgling sounds.

Harand rode into the clearing to find his brother alone and reeling, with blood welling in savage gouts from a raw hole in the middle of his face. He just had time to witness Ring drowning in his own blood, and then his horse collapsed beneath him under a hail of envenomed darts that spat from reed blowpipes invisible to him. Hurling himself from the saddle, Harand somersaulted into the reeds before the darts could do more than stick into his lizard-skin armour. He ran like a hunted animal.

For nearly an hour he ran without stopping, tearing himself and his clothes on branches and briars, muddying himself in streams, and all the while his breath came and went in great sobs of terror. Eventually he collapsed, a heaving bundle of rags and scratches, in a part of the forest where giant trees grew. The Snakeskins would not pursue him far beyond their swampy home. But had he looked up he would have seen the spidery forms of two men straddling the branches above him.

Since Ring and Harand had entered the forest that morning nothing they had done went unobserved by the Forest Folk. It was unfortunate for Harand that he had refused to see these men as more than twigs.

It was difficult to tell quite what happened next; either the tattered heap shifted itself into a cleft in the spreading roots of the great tree nearest, or the roots themselves reached out to clasp the body. In one swift movement a dark spidery shape dropped to a lower branch and hurled a fire-hardened stake into Harand. The other Forester swooped after the spear, adding his own weight to it and pinning the body to the ground. Two branchlike bodies then swung off silently through the treetops.

At the throwing of the spear numerous hooded crows with vicious stone-gray beaks had risen in clamorous spirals from the surrounding trees. Gradually they came wheeling back as the Forest Folk receded. One of the crows flopped down to alight on the stake which pierced the rag-bundle. After a pause it hopped, with a flat grunt, to the body, and its heavy beak prised out an eye.

A few more seconds and no rags, no body were visible—only a mass of black feathers and the stabbing rhythm of gray beaks rising and falling.

9

On the wet window-ledge lay a mound of sand-colored moths; the old man picked them up one by one and held out the furry morsels to a two-foot lizard on the floor. At the offer of each moth a long pale tongue flicked rapidly up and then back into the blank tightness of the creature's jaws. The old man himself, perfectly hairless, was not unlike a lizard, as if through long years of contact he was turning into one of them. Seeming to confirm this, he popped a moth into his own wide mouth from time to time, catching it neatly on the curling point of his tongue. His face sloped back from his lips across a blunt nose with nostrils almost flat against the plane of the face, while his eyes were round and pro-tuberant, constantly flicking about with disconcerting sharpness. The rock floor of the room was covered by two inches of lapping water, and the old man's dark robe, which reached below the surface, had a heavy band of even darker dampness which spread up to about the knee. Nothing in his manner sug-gested that living with this mild flooding was other than normal and, indeed, congenial.

He plucked a ripe snail from the wall and tossed

it into the air so that it fell into the waiting jaws of his companion lizard, which shut with a business-like staccato crunch.

"Guests, my sweet salamander! My endearing dragon! To be precise, guests on quests!"

The old man shook with mirth. Through the window he watched advancing over his causeway, which was sunk just under the surface of the lake, a white boy and a cloaked warrior in a lizard-crested helmet.

"Well he's wearing the right badge for us, eh, my saurian friend? Shall we tell him the truth? Which, though we can put it in all manner of ways, adds up to nothing. What do you suppose he knows about nothing? More than most, I suspect. Have a moth! Here's a juicy death's head. Have another!"

When his guests stood before him Kryll welcomed them to Lizard Lake.

"I knew I should see someone from Tum-Barlum, though I thought it might be after the great cold rather than now. You have many difficulties to face, but you have already achieved much in one sense. Nothing in another. Still, I'm glad they've sent me the one with a wing. Can I look? It's just vulgar curiosity, not, *heh*, wizard's privilege."

Witherwing shook out his wing and submitted it to Kryll's inspection. He found the old man odd, but not offensive; there was too much humor and power implicit in his manner for that. Both these qualities were unsettling, however, and whoever confronted Kryll sensed a superior ironic knowledge which could undermine the worlds of others.

Kryll splashed over to the prince and appraised the magical swan's wing like a tailor.

"Oh very fine, very fine indeed! Now this is quite

some job that they've done on you. If anything were to impress me, this would. But it's all so absurd. Mere playthings!"

"What do you mean?" asked Witherwing.

"Nothing. That is the most truthful and precise answer that I can give you. But now I should be seeing about your comfort. You probably don't like walking in the water and we should dry your feet. It's not quite so nice and damp upstairs, and perhaps we could light a book or two and have a fire."

"You would burn books?" exclaimed Witherwing.

"Oh, I know what's in them, and it's nothing so special. But if you prefer, we'll burn a beam."

"Won't that be dangerous? For the structure, I mean?"

"Got a will of its own, this tower. It would soon tell me if it didn't want me to do it. Fear nothing. *Heh heh!* And then some food, which is more difficult. Wish we could eat books, or get like little grubs into beams. I make do with snacks of snail, you see, and the odd meal of moth. Which is possibly eccentric."

"Don't you eat lizard?" asked Witherwing as they approached the rough stone stairs. Kryll appeared not to hear the question, and Witherwing, looking again at the hairless saurian face, decided not to repeat it. Suddenly he was thankful that he was wearing a tunic over his lizard-skin armor.

At the top of the stairs Kryll turned with unexpected quickness and fixed his eyes upon Hutt, which was the first time the prince had seen them rest upon anything longer than a flickering second or two. The power of concentration was almost palpable. Perhaps Kryll's penetrating vision could match the depths in Hutt's eyes.

"The boy and I, of course, understand each other well enough."

Scooping up a slim white lizard from a recessed ledge, Kryll draped it round his shoulders like a stole and ushered his guests into the upper chamber. Witherwing could make out no ceiling, though at twice a man's height up one side of the wall there projected a platform across almost half the width of the tower, and at the corresponding height above that there was a further platform across the other half. From a yet higher obscurity there was a steady drip of water, a silver thread which terminated with a clocklike *plop-plop-plop* at a puddle in the center of the chamber and then ran discreetly to the side till it reached the doorway and could trickle down to the flood on the floor below. In tottering stacks and scattered heaps books closed them in on all sides. Unfamiliar books with yellow pages that could not have been made from the skin of the fat-rabbit. Books with little gardens of fungus and moss sprouting from cases which appeared of unparalleled magnificence to Witherwing. Books which opened on pages of dense inscrutable hieroglyphs. The prince was awed: No wonder this man was called deep-minded Kryll.

One pile of books keeled over into the central puddle as Kryll cleared a space near the window. With careless abandon he tore several volumes to pieces, bundled them together on the floor, and with a candle eventually ignited the damp pages. When Witherwing protested, bewildered and hesitating, Kryll said:

"They're all called *The Art of Dying*. None of them are true. None of them real. Sit down and get warm."

He motioned to book-stacks that would make

convenient seats and, with the smoke gathering about them, they approached the flames. *Slap-slap-slap*—the silver thread dropped on to a gold-tooled book cover.

"Eat this," said Kryll, holding out some gray leathery slabs. "It's fish. Tastes just like books."

"What do the lizards eat?" Witherwing asked as the creature on Kryll's shoulder began to nuzzle his ear.

"Anything. Rats, frogs, insects, fish. Each other."

Witherwing found it hard to adjust to Kryll's manner, for he had expected stiff formality and ritual from one who had a reputation for wizardry. The habit of irony was almost unknown to him and his people, and he felt at a disadvantage—but not hostile, for he was sure that there was much to be learned here.

"Witherwing. So you are he. Now what's in a name? Born, perhaps, with a withered arm, so they take you off and fix you up with the help of a swan? Or possibly only a pun for one born with-a-wing. It would fit them. Games, games. *Heh-heh-heh!*"

Kryll's laugh was all breath and no voice. Witherwing kept silent, partly because the ramifications of the questions were beyond him, partly because he sensed that Kryll was only going over ground in his own mind, and did not expect a response.

"You have come here, have been sent—as I expected someone to be sent—to seek my help. Why was it you, the youngest? Do they want you to succeed? Do they want you back? You are going to Karn-Ingli in search of what? Power. Led by something less than a tale in an old book like this."

Kryll tossed another volume on the fire.

"A tale of glowing stones in the Upper Lands

from a traveller. Who was he? Perhaps they sent him."

"You mean Hrasp holds out for me the bait of the glowing stones?" asked Witherwing.

"I told you nothing of Hrasp-the-Hunter, but this I will tell you: If I were one of your bards, then I would say that Hrasp is your perfect enemy and that tales of your combats will enliven many a firelit feast in hall. And he *is* your enemy, and he might kill you. But I am not one of your bards, and life is not a tale. Though there are many besides bards that would make it so."

"You talk of 'they,'" Witherwing said, "and I don't know them. You talk of 'sending,' yet not of who sends."

"True indeed, my feathered friend. But I shall help you. I shall take you above, and I shall take you below, and tell you what could lead you to the truth. If you are warmer and drier now, let's go up."

Having adjusted the somnolent lizard around his neck, Kryll led the way to the steps at the wall, recklessly scattering books as he went. They ascended from platform to platform, there being three more than the two that had been visible from the chamber of books, until they arrived at the bird-clustered parapet and looked down on the lake. The lizards bunched on the rocks appeared not to have moved at all, and Witherwing had the impression that their ritualistically upturned heads were all pointed toward the black tower. A white line, a cloud of mist, and an unearthly roar told where the waterfall dropped from the table of this lake. In the direction of Karn-Ingli the towering Manfish Mountain curved around the waters and cast a chill and splintered reflection on the surface. Kryll pointed to a wisp of white smoke, almost imperceptible against its snowy background, on the shore beneath the mountain. A white bird settled tamely on his outstretched hand, while another fluttered on to his bald head.

"Look carefully."

At first Witherwing could see nothing beside the smoke, but then it was as if a small mound of snow had heaved itself and begun to busy itself with the fire—now another mound, and Witherwing knew that he was looking at furclad Karns like those that had been waiting for him when he entered the foothills. As final confirmation a dark figure, dressed in the blue skin of the manfish, appeared over a ridge and joined the two at the fire.

"It's you they're waiting for," said Kryll. "They know you're here, and they know what you did for their friends. While you're here they won't come after you. Because I'm a *heh-heh-heh,* a magician."

"Do I fight those warriors?" Witherwing inquired.

"No. I shall show you a way. Once you're past them you must tackle Manfish Mountain, climbing up the nose end there, where at least it's not a precipice. On the other side you'll have a few days through the passes before you reach the ice peaks, where there are eternal snows. The passes will be covered now, but you'll find a passage, and you'll even meet some friends of mine. You must spend some time with them because they will teach you to survive the eternal snows."

"Have I passed through furbeast country yet?"

"No. They're not usually seen till Manfish Mountain and beyond. Use the boy here and you'll be all right. Otherwise, it will depend upon you and your own fears. The furbeast uses you against yourself; he never touches his prey before it's dead, and there is no death more terrible than that which he brings about. I'll give you maps; they'll be of some use to you some of the time."

Witherwing gazed up at the cold slopes, knowing that what he had endured up to now was as nothing compared to the dangers which lay ahead.

"Now let's go below," said Kryll.

The bedrock of the tower was not, like the first floor, flooded, though all surfaces were permanently damp. At the center of the gloomy basement chamber, which was lit by one small square opening up a high chute, was a perfectly circular hole that looked like a well. What the purpose could be of a well in the middle of a lake was unknown to Witherwing.

"Come to the edge. Right up," said Kryll, and they stood around the unguarded rim of the great black hole of unknowable depth.

"Is the tower built on a rock?" the hairless old man went on. "Not really. Built on a hole—black hole where you thought a heart might be. *Heh-heh-heh!* What are you after? Glowing stones you call them. Which are . . . what? Power . . . and death. Only death is certain. Power is just one way of death. All power is a scent of death in the nostrils, and it is not your path, yet you seem to pursue it. Lean out now—over the hole—and I will tell you—" the words came all breath again, no voice, like a lizard—"the secret of life. Which is no secret, which is nothing. Death. We never move from the lip of the pit until we fall . . . into nothing. Death is not outstripped. Death is no man in black, nothing to be met, nothing to meet. Go on your quest. Nothing matters. Nothing."

The whisper echoed and dwindled down the hole. Then Kryll spoke again:

"Not even my lovely lizards."

Witherwing saw a white streak as Kryll heaved

109

the creature from his shoulders into the pit, and the three figures bent their ears to the space and waited. Waited. Waited for the sound of the body striking rock or water. Waited without drawing breath. Waited, but no sound came. Nothing.

At last Kryll looked up and said:

"See into the boy's mind. Use it."

But Witherwing had seen pits enough.

"I know. I know," he said, and his thoughts, all estranged, turned to the eternal snows.

10

Before dawn Witherwing awoke to a stertorous rushing noise as of fire and wind. The whole lake seemed in tumult, yet not a breeze touched his cheek, and he could see nothing through the window when he left his bed of tumbled books. His fingers stuck to the ice-covered ledge, and time lost all meaning for him in this nightmare world of hissing and darkness. The sound neither rose nor fell; it was steady, hypnotic, appalling.

So Witherwing did not know how long he stood at the tower's dark window, but when the misty rays of pre-dawn light appeared his beard was white with frost while his hand, dangerously numb, could only be removed from the frozen stone by repeated warm breaths upon the ice. Gray shapes in the wolf-light resolved themselves into lizard-clustered rocks. Still the animals had not moved, but lay with heads raised toward the tower. The lake itself seemed to have shrunk, and gradually Witherwing perceived that during the night ice had formed around the shores, except where the great falls continued to pour white water now mixed with small ice-floes.

A thread of fire outlined Manfish Mountain as the sky grew pink. Then the sun broke over its summit and rosy streamers tumbled like water down the side of the mountain, dashing blue shadows into crevasses. The sun itself stood behind a fringe of mountain-top trees from which all snow had been knifed away by winds from, the Upper Lands, with the result that they now stood encased, in all their detail, in thin bright ice; stars, splinters, sparks and flames burst from the glassy branches as the sun rolled up behind them. All in one moment Lizard Lake was splashed with gold, and Kryll's ice-plated black tower burned on the brazen surface. And the lizards burned too, with orange gleams on their white armored skins.

The lizards! Now the dry hissing which filled the air was explained. Every lizard mouth was open and from every throat rushed air that did not vibrate on vocal tissue—voices of ghosts.

Suddenly it stopped. The whole tableau held itself like an indrawn breath. Then a man-size lizard slid from his rock and rippled the molten surface of the lake. Others began to do the same, quietly dropping into the water and following the first toward a headland on the lake's mountain shore. A silent procession of lustrous white lizard heads passed before Kryll's tower under the wondering gaze of Witherwing.

"Down for another half-year," wheezed Kryll, plucking Witherwing from his reverie. "No, don't turn. Watch them go."

As the head of the leading lizard approached the lake's ice-bound fringe it sank suddenly from view and did not reappear. Those immediately behind took up the cue, and so it was repeated all down the great wedge-shaped flotilla until only a bright spreading eddy marked for a while where the flat white heads had been.

"Farewell my sweet scaly friends!" cried out Kryll. "I'll see you all green again at spring o' the leaf."

Kryll turned his back on the window, blew on his white fingers and rubbed them vigorously together. His joints crackled like icicles.

"*Heh!* And now dear bird, and you, pale peach of a boy, let me look after you. Here's a book cries out to be burnt. Let's have a fire. And then I shall cook for you—and if that's not a deep-minded wonder then, *heh-heh-heh*, nothing is."

Having stoked up a good paper blaze the old lizard man produced a black iron pan from a book-piled corner and proceeded to heat it. He dropped into it three lumps of fat, each about the size of a snail, which spattered merrily as they skated over the hot metal. From the top of the window he broke a couple of icicles into a pot and reduced them over the flames back to water, into which he poured a white powder from a twist of paper. Almost at once the mixture frothed into a dough, which increased in volume with alarming rapidity. Kryll whisked a handful off the overflowing bowl and dropped the doughball into the pan, where it continued to grow as it began to turn appetizingly light brown. Six such balls filled the pan to capacity and Kryll gave his attention to them, soon losing the unwashed mixing-pot under a fresh bookfall. After a few moments of prodding into the steaming meal he darted like a lizard to some inscrutable book-covered storage place, and returned with a jug of clear golden honey, which he emptied over the fried globes of dough. Deftly he flipped two of the brown syrupy delights on to a leatherbound volume which he proffered to Hutt. Then two for Witherwing, and two for himself.

Witherwing had some misgivings about the fat used for frying, but one who is particular about his food could make no traveller, so he ate, and ate heartily, finding after the first mouthful that deep-minded Kryll had truly worked a wonder.

Witherwing told him so.

"Ah, thank you, dear wing! I don't dare to think what age those ingredients might be. But then, one year is much like another, and my lizards will be back when the ice melts again. They've taken to the caves now—as, indeed, you will shortly. I've thought of going down myself for the half-year, but," and here he gestured round the cold, chaotic chamber, "I'd miss my home comforts."

"I, er, um," began Witherwing, momentarily at a loss. "I, er, suppose there would be no books there?"

"Books? Ah yes. Burn 'em up! Burn 'em up! The word takes fire, eh! So it should. Offer them up, burning words, to the empty sky. Very fitting. *Heh-heh-heh.*"

Two more volumes landed in the flames, their damp yellow pages turning orange and black.

"I would give much to learn what these books say," said Witherwing. "Great wisdom must be in them."

"I suppose you want to suggest that I teach you to read them?" was Kryll's sharp response.

"No. That would be burdensome to ask, or to accept. But I should like to . . . *know.*"

"I wouldn't teach you anyway. Literature breeds distress. Thirst for learning is thirst for power, and power is death. These things are axiomatic. Not *entirely* true. But axiomatic. Knowledge and power have burned the world. We're only scab-dwellers. Ah, but keep your mind on Hrasp. Let's stay with dreams and heroic melancholy. You have tasks to perform, battles to fight, and I must play my part. Use the boy"—he glanced at Hutt's white face—"as long as you can. He's more reliable than anything I can give. As long as you can."

Kryll drifted about for a short while through valleys of books.

"Just as well, really, you're here. At a loss, you know, without my lizards. I don't do anything. Haven't for a long time. It's the best way, but I like to do nothing with my lizards."

He rubbed his hands and cracked his joints.

"And now let me cook for you!"

"But you have just done that."

"Quite. Quite. *Heh-heh*. Now where's that pan . . . ?"

Witherwing rolled most of this installment of honeyed doughballs beneath some neighboring books, while Hutt made no pretence of eating his. Kryll did not heed these things, nor his own share of the food, which he quickly lost, together with the pan, soon after he had dislodged a magnificent icicle from the window by throwing one of his confections, with an action unexpectedly swift and accurate as a lizard's tongue.

"Time to play," he said. "I must have my play. Come too if you like."

Hauling a squat wooden chair, alive with sinuous lizard carvings, down the steps, Kryll lurched to the floor below, which now had a carpet of thick smooth ice. Witherwing, still unsure how to plumb this deep man's mind, watched him hurl the heavy chair so that it skidded across the ringing ice and sharply struck the wall opposite. As it rebounded, spinning, Kryll threw his arms into the air and launched himself with seeming abandon on to the glassy floor, over which he slid with breathtaking speed to land with a triumphant shout in the still spinning chair. His tucked-up legs slapped against the stone wall and immediately straightened to send the chair rocketing insanely back across the ice. *Slap!* A great lizard grin flashed with dizzying rotation back and forth. *Slap! Slap!* Crazily complex arabesques were scraped over the surface, and white ice-stars spurted out like sprays of mountain flowers behind the eye-defying chair. Above the hissing of wood on ice came another hiss which reminded Witherwing of his chill morning vigil at the window, and as Kryll's hairless head flickered from wall to wall in a white blur, he could just see that its long and lipless mouth was taut and open.

Witherwing returned to the chamber of books and stared across the empty lake. Like shadows, images of home floated beneath his thought. The High Hall of Rumi, his father; his brothers, from whom he felt separate irrespective of his physical distance from them; tales of the bards, in which he had seemed to live before confronting the all-embracing negative which was Hutt's power and the cryptic utterances of this wizard Kryll; the fierce green and red splendor of his Snakeskin lover, and the wind-earth-and-stars beauty of Nada the Flatlander.

Below him the echoing scrapes, slaps, cracks, and hisses of Kryll's play reverberated unheeded as the sun passed on its low course through the morning.

At midday Kryll mounted the stairs, the stout carved chair bumping along behind him. He lit a few books, and put the chair on the blaze. Smoke thickened inside the tower and drops of water splashed down from unseen melting icicles. In this eerie atmosphere the old man began to instruct Witherwing in the journey that lay before him, producing maps of a richness of detail unfamiliar to the prince. He explained that Witherwing must take time to learn how to survive in the eternal snows, and how he would put him in the care of a people who dwelt beyond Manfish Mountain to accomplish this. From there the prince would be guided by a needle on a cord in addition to his maps; it would point, even over vast distances, directly to the valley of clouds which was Karn-Ingli. Smoke-shrouded Kryll passed over to him this needle of heavy dull gray metal. This was true wizardry! Not even the bards of Tum-Barlum had told of these magic metal fingers.

"Not so magical, but just as necessary—some food. Fish. That tastes like book covers. But doesn't burn so well."

He handed over some of the dull leathery slabs, like those that Hutt and Witherwing had sampled on their first arrival, and a light bundle of sticks and skins which could be made into a serviceable tent.

"And now, so as to skirt those manfish-hunters, those . . . those . . . *lizard-eaters*, it's time you went . . . *down!*"

The lizard-faced wonder-worker rose to his full height in the swirling smoke and clapped his hands as he pronounced the last word. His black sleeves shook like crow's wings.

"*Nothing* to fear. Heh-heh-heh!"

Kryll led Witherwing and Hutt down to the icy floor scored by his morning's play, then down again to the dark bedrock and the central well.

"But this has no end!" exclaimed Witherwing as they stood at the lip of the black circle.

"Let's not be too absolute about this," said Kryll. "We'll have a quest, an adventure, instead. Look at the iron staples."

From the ragged sleeve of his robe Kryll

plucked a long coarse thread, which he tied round the middle of his lighted candle-stump. This he lowered some way down the cylindrical pit, and, just before the flame licked up and bit through the black thread, Witherwing glimpsed the rusty staples which descended regularly into the obscurity where the candle disappeared.

"About two hundred you need to go down, where you'll find a tunnel, a bit bigger than this, that leads off horizontally. Take it and don't leave it till you come out behind the Karns. If you meet any of my lizards, well . . . take care. Greet for me my friends over the mountain, but tell them not to come and fish through the lake's ice too soon, not till Hrasp's men have gone. Farewell, white one. And you, dear wing, come back when you can, perhaps when the lizards return. But bring none of your glowing stones near me. I'm sure your battles will be all that the bards could wish, and possibly the eternal snows will not drive out the green and gold bardic glory that drapes your mind."

Witherwing gave a grand feathery salute and thanked Kryll in the forms of Tum-Barlum, though his words did not seem to him to fit the lizard magician; but he knew no others, and Kryll appeared pleased enough—especially with the flourish of the wing. Then he lowered himself over the edge of the pit and began to descend, using the iron rungs. Hutt followed him. Swiftly the icy walls of the cylinder closed on them as the pale gray disc of light above diminished. The silhouette of Kryll's hairless head broke into this disc, and his dry voice echoed down the hole.

"By the way, you might, after all, fancy a book. I shouldn't believe a word of it, if I were you. Well,

I don't suppose you will, since you probably won't be able to read it. Catch!"

The book began to flutter down with increasing speed. Witherwing spread his wing wide and netted it, for it would have been impossible to have snatched it by hand in this gloom. Supporting himself on his wing, which stretched right across the tunnel, Witherwing stowed the diminutive limp-covered volume in a pocket beneath his cloak, called up his thanks, and climbed downward again.

"Also by the way—*you're being followed, of course ... Heh-heh-heh ...*"

Kryll's saurian head drew back from the pit, and his chuckles were a long time fading away.

11

King Rumi sat shadowed deep in the throne of
his High Hall, his brows wreathed with the ivy-
leaves of mourning. His court, similarly wreathed,
was a knot of red, brown and gold, pressed close
around the great fire. Harand and Ring had been giv-
en up for dead, and the bard was about to make
their history. The droneharp was struck, the bard's
voice intoned:

> Weight of great sorrow lies on us after our wait
> Suns rise in vain when a land is robbed of its king's
>   sons
> Sore are the days since Harand and Ring we last saw
> No brighter war-deeds than theirs shall we know
> Sword in hand like eagles to battle they soared
> Bare is the High Hall now arms they no longer bear
> Boughs of the forest shall grieve them, the tall
>   mountain bows
> Leaves fall to the ground when a prince's soul leaves
> Sure we are waves weep for them on the gray shore
> Mist comes in tear-clouds to say they are missed.

12

"... *you're being followed ... you're being followed ...*"

The words thumped in Witherwing's mind at each rusty iron rung. That cryptic old lizard man seemed, he thought, to take a mischievous delight in such sudden sallies that put one at a puzzled disadvantage. For all Kryll's dismissive attitude toward power, he had his sly and witty way of controlling people, as Witherwing had now begun to realize.

"What does he mean me to do about it?" asked the prince aloud.

Unexpectedly Hutt broke into his consciousness. He should have thought of the boy's power. Now there formed in him the image of a vast and dusty plain beneath a flat sky of dull yellow from which a few flecks of snow were blown by a scouring desolate wind. And far, far in the distance a figure faced Witherwing, unrecognizable but purposeful. All that lonely scene was imbued with a melancholy yearning; no hostility, no danger rose from it.

The image changed. Witherwing felt himself

moving inexorably from darkness toward a distant white spot which grew and grew until terror and vacuity made up his whole being, so that a final, ghastly, obliterating explosion seemed imminent. Suddenly it was over, and there was nothing. Hutt's mind disengaged from his, leaving Witherwing to ponder on how often he had been led to brinks recently, there to have revealed to him . . . nothing.

And even as this thought occurred to him, his foot, where he had expected it to land on another iron staple, waved in empty air, almost causing Witherwing to lose his balance. With a powerful flap of his wing he steadied himself and stretched downward and from side to side with his foot, thereby discovering that he had reached the tunnel which ran off at right angles from that which he and Hutt were descending. Aided again by a thrust of his wing, he was able to swing his body into the new tunnel, to the relief of his strained arm and legs. He leaned out and clutched Hutt's arm, and so drew him from the vertical shaft. Hutt could walk upright here, but it was necessary for Witherwing to stoop somewhat, even after he had removed his lizard-crested helmet. At first this was no inconvenience, so buoyed was he with being able to walk on the level, but it was not long before his neck and shoulders began to ache wearily, and he grew angry with himself for the increasing frequency with which he cracked his head against the cold, encrusted tunnel roof. Sense of time and sense of distance became confused, for they walked, after a few minutes of candlelight, in darkness, and there were no bends in the passage.

Witherwing's frustrating disorientation prevented him from hearing the sounds as soon as he should have done, so that when he stopped, alert and with a knife already tight in his fist, he could not have been more than ten paces from whatever it was. There was not much sound at all; something sluggish and heavy was suggested, almost as if the circumference of the tunnel was about to become a massive devouring maw, ready to grind him and the boy and gulp them back into intestine labyrinths beyond. The sounds, when they came, were disgusting: lumpen squeezings, coarse scrapings, and vile salivation. But nothing approached Witherwing, so after some tense minutes he decided that what lay ahead was not aware of his presence, was perhaps animate only in the way of a vegetable. The last possibility did not lessen his alarm, for he was familiar with some of the flesh-eating fungi of the deep forest bordering Tum-Barlum. As a boy he had witnessed, during a pigrat hunt, one of his father's men enfolded by a crusty, orange, spongelike monstrosity against which he had carelessly leaned. Stinging juices had begun to eat him even before the bubbling growth had covered him. The horror of hearing muffled screams from within the fungus had been paralyzing to the boy. Now Witherwing was set to see a fungoid orifice before him as he quietly sheathed his blade and prepared to strike a light.

He was almost disappointed when, by the first brief flashes of his flint, he saw that the passage ahead was clear. Almost clear. As the candle flame quivered into life there was revealed a white shape carpeting the way ahead. It was one of Kryll's lizards, huge . . . and with two heads. There could be no mistake—four eyes glinted up at him in the candlelight. A minor convulsion ensued, during which the forward head drew back a little, and Witherwing knew that he was looking at one lizard in the last stages of swallowing another. Both were still alive and were taking a long and almost disinterested time over the process. The swallower's jaws stretched appallingly wide into what seemed a terrible grin, and his meal looked up at Witherwing, opening his mouth from which there burbled a dry, cracked hiss.

There was some consolation in the fact that Witherwing had only to combat his own repulsion, for the lizards were in no position to offer a threat to him. It would be unworthy of him to do violence to the creatures, yet he longed for mind-numbing action that might exorcise the dread that this sight aroused in him. The lack of drama in the sordid scene conveyed an unwelcome vision of life to a prince on an heroic quest. Holding his candle aloft, Witherwing strode up to the beasts and planted his foot on the neck of the eater, causing the eaten to hiss and make an uncoordinated and ineffective attempt to snap at the man who continued to walk firmly down the armored back, from which he alighted with no more than a weak but angry slap on his leg from the lizard's tail. When Hutt crossed in the same way the animals made no movement at all— not a breath, nor a flicker of the eye.

The flame revealed that there were fissures in the tunnel walls, some barely hairline cracks, others substantial cave-passages. Down some of the latter Witherwing observed further lizards following the same dull, sightless, meaningless round as the predator and prey he had passed. Once he saw a male in the marginally diminished lethargy of his sexual excitement mount another-male; neither seemed able to work out what had gone wrong, and for a long time their hisses and leathery thwacks reverberated after Witherwing and Hutt.

A descent so deep into the earth might have

been expected to furnish the most wondrous dangers, but the journey was proving almost as uneventful as the passage was straight and long. By the time the tunnel began to incline upward the lizards had been left far behind and there was no evidence, despite Kryll's last chuckling words, that they were being followed, or that any threatening presence lay ahead. Gradually the air grew fresher, and a faint luminosity appeared above and before them which increased slowly until Witherwing found himself bursting wing-first through the drift of soft snow plugging the end of the tunnel. Over them hung a large flat rock, which would obscure the tunnel's entrance when the snow did not, and Hutt and Witherwing had to squeeze through like lizards before they were truly in the open. They climbed up the bank from which the rock projected to look back across the frozen lake, diamond bright in the sunlight that assailed their darkness-accustomed eyes, to Kryll's black tower, and, nearer to them, the encampment of Hrasp's warriors.

"So we've slipped by them under their very feet!" exulted Witherwing, refreshed by the bright open world before him.

But Hrasp's men all heard the dagger-sharp screams of Witherwing as he turned away from them.

Where he had expected to see the white hump of Manfish Mountain and a free expanse of blue sky, the prince was confronted by a nightmare more smothering than any underground cave. The sky had slammed shut like a lid of black razors, and the man became less than a baby in understanding. This was terror so pure that he had no defense—forgot his sword, his wing, forgot all but a seed of self threatened by the blackest enormity. Leather wings burst his hearing, and his own long screams were part of a clawing horror that raked his body so deep that he seemed to have ripped through the thin wall of death, which he would have welcomed, to an unimaginable beyond.

He was plunged so deep in pain, and yet he knew there was no limit; the end was already passed, and torment swelled infinitely beyond the end. Over it all, on a rippling curtain of blood, hovered the mockery. Cancerous white, two glittering points of death, thin red lips of the bitterest laughter. Laughter, because the sharpest bite was yet to come —and even when a deeper agony. This laughter stabbed like thorns into eyeballs and slashed like arrows through a ribboned body.

Then a white path opened up like morning through the horror, and Witherwing knew that Hutt had beamed his power on the nightmare, which shrank until a cringing, shaggy, apelike figure shambled off into the snows. This was the furbeast that had nearly caused Witherwing to die of fright. A slack-jawed, slavering creature, he had little physical strength, but he acted as a mirror in which men met their deepest fears and died in their embrace. After which the beast would regale himself with steaming flesh before the body froze.

Heedless of the danger from the Karns, who would surely investigate, Witherwing hung his head and waited for the convulsions which he knew would come. Twice his body heaved helplessly while racking breaths came long and shuddering. Then he fell moaning in the snow, where he made weak twitching movements from time to time. As consciousness ebbed back he became aware that the Karns were in some kind of difficulty, and he almost fell senseless again when he realized from the pitch of their screams that they had now fallen prey to the furbeast. And they did not have Hutt.

"I should be many times dead without you, boy," he said. "Can I ever make return?"

"Nada," said Hutt.

This was his first and last word to Witherwing.

The boy was standing a little above Witherwing, with his face toward Manfish Mountain. The prince stood where he had fallen, looking up to the boy, whose eyes gazed forward into nothing. Suddenly there was a small movement in those eyes, impossible for the prince to decipher, until the air sang and a heavy white spear hurtled into Hutt's breast and threw him dead in the snow where spreading crimson soon glistened with the white.

Witherwing tore out his sword and spun round with the springlike tension of a forest animal to see, at some distance from him on a snowy crest, a powerful figure astride a matted snowbull. For a moment, mount and rider were still and statuesque against the radiant sky, the man staring down at Witherwing so that the prince could see the full spread of antlers which branched from his temples.

The great horned head was thrown back, and a deep rolling laugh came down to Witherwing as Hrasp-the-Hunter turned the face of his snowbull toward the mountain and disappeared without haste behind the ridge from which he had thrown his spear.

13

Hutt must have foreseen his death, and even if that were not so then he still would have seen Hrasp rising above the snowbank, the antlers, followed by the bulk of his body and that of the snowbull, the strong arm aloft, and the swift hurl of the bone spear. Yet he had done nothing; had not avoided the confrontation, had not warned Witherwing, had not used the destructive power of his mind that the prince had seen awesomely displayed against their would-be attackers before, had made not the slightest movement to evade the spear which, at that distance, might easily have been dodged. It had seemed like a surrender to destiny. Though Hrasp-the-Hunter was known to be formidable, his force was surely brutish compared with that of the pale boy, and, whatever tales there were of his unaccountable longevity, magical powers of mind were not held to be among his attributes. Hutt had seemed to know that Witherwing himself had been in no danger on this occasion, for, though beyond emotion, the boy had been unfailingly efficient in serving the prince's interest. He had saved him from the terror of the furbeast—why then had he immediately given himself up to death and abandoned Witherwing's quest?

For the dangers could not be over. With the deadly and mocking eruption of Hrasp himself on the scene they might have just begun. And then there were Kryll's words, "You're being followed," which, from the mysterious image that had been communicated to Witherwing through Hutt's mind, did not seem to refer to Hrasp-the-Hunter.

Should the furbeast return, Witherwing would have no defense against it, and he shuddered again at the possibility. That a grotesque, shambling, slobbering parody of a man should be able to destroy a warrior by a fear which burned! It did not occur to the winged prince of a world which seemed old, yet had so little known history, that part of the furbeast's horror came simply from the fact that he was such a parody.

The prince stood alone in this cold white world, his magnificent wing, which could sometimes express the godlike freedom of the air, drooping like a tumbled cloth. Life continued to be a relentless process of stripping away. The greater the power of perception, like Hutt's, the more this view was confirmed. Such was his weariness he might have welcomed death, and he was tempted to lie down and simply wait for the delicious warmth that is supposed to come at last to the man dying of cold. But something in him rejected this solution, and instead he began to drag himself up the snowy slope toward Manfish Mountain. He felt only that he should climb the mountain and, hopefully, perish with the effort, for he had no thought of his quest in the lands that lay beyond. Death must overtake him while he struggled; he would not passively await it.

With the help of his sword, Witherwing scooped out a deep hole in the snow in which he laid the frail body of Hutt. With his pale skin and hair the boy seemed to belong in this white grave, rather than in the brown earth of his Flatland home. At last his profound eyes were closed, and Witherwing hoped that meant peace, not that the boy had merely retreated into other empty worlds. Soft top-snow flowed in the winds that blew out of the ice-peaks of the Upper Lands, so that Hutt's grave was all but indistinguishable by the time that Wither-wing had trudged to the top of the first ridge that lay in the direction of Manfish Mountain. Here he turned and looked back down his own ragged tracks that were being speedily effaced, across Hutt's grave, over the grisly remains of the furbeast's feast upon the Karns, to the huge slab of Lizard Lake and Kryll's snow-dusted tower, assertive as if it were anchored to the core of the earth itself. Witherwing saw in the now fading light of the afternoon that a fire had been kindled on the parapet of the tower, and he could just make out the black figure of Kryll him-self feeding the flames, with books, presumably. His white birds scattered like ash from the heat. As the orange flames surged higher, Witherwing sensed that Kryll was looking directly at him, and that the hardly perceptible motions of the wonder-worker were beckoning him back. The sky had turned a dull and uniform yellow. Witherwing's mind, weak from the shocks of the day, seemed to ring with threatening metallic waves; it was as if he fell into a dream, as from the fire-tipped tower emerged a tiny figure walking purposefully in his direction, first on the ice round the tower then over what must have been another sunken causeway, while the wind whipped at its garments. Thrumming through the prince's head came Kryll's last words . . .

Without thought Witherwing stumbled back the way he had just climbed, not even pausing where he had buried Hutt. He passed unseeing by the mutilated bodies of the Karns, which were still partially exposed, and on he dragged, as if desperate to meet the approaching figure before it left the surface of the lake. Kryll, from the top of his tower, watched the two small bodies, in all that white expanse, come face to face on the windy surface of the lake.

"*Nada!*" cried Witherwing, gazing on the brown-flecked beauty of Hutt's sister. His exclamation, cracked with pain though it was, made it clear that he had met with the only relief in a hopeless world. Folded together they moved across the ice and water back to Kryll's tower, where they passed the night in the room of books. He lay still in her arms all night, and not till dawn had broken did he stroke the dark burning glow of her hair, did he kiss her honey-freckled breasts, did he wrap her whole sweet body in his godlike wing.

"He called me," said Nada, "almost as soon as you had left. And I could see then it was because he knew he should die and he knew when. I felt it when he died too. Not any pain, but he just let go of me, stopped directing me. He was telling me I had arrived."

"But have you made such a journey alone? I should not have come this far without the boy."

Witherwing cradled again her strong brown body in feathers.

"In a sense he was with me, too," she said. "But no; kinsmen brought me through the hills and black pines, and now they have returned to the Flatlands. When those with the power call they are not refused

131

among our people, even though, as now, we cannot see the end. You shall do something yet that will touch the lives of all of us, however much that old wizard tells us that actions are no more than ashes."

"Well, he cooks a breakfast that's marginally better than ashes, and I think that's what he's about now. He dries a fish however, that is rather worse."

Somewhere beyond a range of bookhills Kryll was repeating his performances with the iron pan and expanding doughballs, singing the while an obviously extemporized song about his lizards "with their scales of snow, in the dark caves far below." Nada and Witherwing quietly twined their limbs together; so deep had they gone into each other that the old lizard man, his tower, and the white world beyond ceased to exist for them.

"Ah dear duck," said Kryll after breakfast, "poor wing! What a world! If it's all for nothing, then why such pain? That's what you want to ask."

"No," replied the prince.

"For the first time, I confess it, you surprise me. Just a little. See, let me express it by raising my . . . skin where my eyebrows might be, by rolling my eyes—*roll, roll*—by shaping the mouth to a tight round O, and casting my arms in the air."

With manic relish he performed all these actions.

"And what will you 'do now?" he asked, his tongue flicking sharply in and out. "Go back and live with the Flatlanders, or back to your father's High Hall with a new and fine princess? Hrasp has already pillaged a few border earthcamps of the Flatlanders—you saw him on his return, though his raiding party will take a longer route to carry their booty back to Karn-Ingli. They drive the herds as far as they can and slaughter them where the land freezes; then they use snowbull sleds for the rest of the way. And that's no small undertaking. So they won't return to the Flatlands for a year. They hardly needed to go there at all this time, except to remind Flatlanders of what life is like. Anyway it'll be safe for you to return now."

"No," said Witherwing again. "Kryll, I am not now much interested in ends or reasons, but I shall follow the horned oaf that killed the boy. Should I go back to Tum-Barlum I could not hear with patience the bards make of this a tale where all fits, which points to some end which I know to be false. I shall struggle with these fragments myself, and not as in a tale. Nada has told me that this is what I should do, and my way is with Nada."

"Truer than you know, my blessed birdie," muttered Kryll reflectively. "Well, you have your tent and your dried fish, you know your way to my friends over the mountain, you have clothes, weapons, and each other. The world is all before you. And a cold one it is, too."

14

There were three generations in the house under the snow, the grandfather and grandmother being called simply The Man and The Woman. Both had entered senility and were swollen with goiter, so that soon their rations would be reduced and they themselves would deliberately occupy the colder parts of the house, and so die. Fish, their son, would then become The Man, and the first of his two wives, who was also his sister, The Woman. These wives were called Fox and Gull, and each had borne a child, one called Dog, the other Lizard. In the village of snowdwellers the family of Fish was regarded as particularly flourishing, for here the man who sired one child in his lifetime could count himself lucky, and Fox was now heavy with another baby. Here at the skirts of the lands of eternal snow was a dying people, and when for a short and fierce season the snows withdrew from these passes there was always another derelict dwelling to join those which already made up more than half the village. Where once Hrasp's men had indulged in full-scale plunder every few years, there were now only odd cases of rape or robbery of livestock committed by stragglers from Karn-Ingli.

When Witherwing and Nada had come to this snow-choked pass in the bright stillness of dawn, after an icy night on the slopes of Manfish Mountain, they did not think of death and dereliction. The world seemed to them a vast silvery bowl brimming with potential wonder, transcending the violence which they had faced and had yet to encounter. It was not a case of pushing away unpleasant thoughts, but of having their beings flooded with light from a loftier, stranger world. Eternity seemed to have dropped its hem where they stood. Almost unmoving veils of pink smoke hung in the air above the buried village which was their destination.

The villagers had proved to be kindly, open people in spite of their enclosed and burrowlike manner of life; their treatment of the senile did not rise from any spirit of bitterness, and there appeared to be no resentment on either side. It was obvious that they held Kryll in high esteem, and Fish saw it as a mark of special favor that he had been chosen by the wonder-worker as host and instructor to the hero with a wing. Fish's people were beardless with tanned leathery skin and dark glinting slits of eyes to cope with their world of dazzling snow alternating with the twilight of their homes. They dressed in heavy skins and furs, and had long thick yellow hair which they greased with animal fat. So much did they love noise and chatter and tumbling over each other in their confined undersnow house that it seemed pleasantly fitting to Witherwing that they should take animal names. The animals they kept, which included two large milk-giving goats, some great white dogs, and a few small but hardy fowl, lived simply as part of the family; they ate, played, quarrelled and slept together. At first it had seemed as though Witherwing might just as well have spoken with the animals as with Fish, Fox, or Gull, but gradually his ear grew attuned to their manner of speech and he recognized that their language differed from his mainly in pronunciation.

Nada and the prince, in all the toppling confusion of this communal life, were respectfully accorded independence and solitude to a degree unprecedented in such a household. Not that it was much by other standards, but they were grateful for it and enjoyed all the more their involvement with the family. Eventually they even grew used to the thick smell that enwreathed the house of Fish, to which diet, lack of washing, animals, the skins used for clothes, all contributed significantly. They slept apart from the family in sweet dried grasses gathered from Manfish Mountain in the warm season and laid on the massive pile of logs which, together with animal dung, served for fuel through the time of snow. For many days they were content to be buried together in this way, taking no thought for subsequent duties and action. In the midst of death, emptiness, and cold they had found a warm retreat. Love spread open roads between them, and Fish and his family felt as if they had been visited by a divinity.

"See, they glow," Fish told his wives. "This is god's fire. Perhaps you need a wing to fly and snatch it. But I don't think so," and here he snatched at them and laughed uproariously. "For there's only two of them, and there's plenty of us."

And Fish tumbled his round-bellied Fox and passionately athletic Gull together in a long and rolling and roaring embrace; with laughter and sighs and deep sucking kisses they frolicked over their bed of furs, and white dogs came barking merry encouragement and licking what faces they could find, while Dog and Lizard, squealing with delight, romped naked among the warm press of their parents' bodies. Nada and Witherwing, in the swell of their own time-cancelling embrace, were swept up by all this jubilance. The goats nuzzled each other in the dark and chewed quietly, while The Man and The Woman smiled toothlessly, moved away from the warmth.

So weeks passed like a kiss, and in that time Nada and Witherwing rarely climbed the ladder from the warm dim home into the frosty brilliance of the upper air. But when they did, the world was still a wonder to them: such cold and such snow were like the pure sharp wit of a divine jest.

Then one morning, as family and guests were drinking together a warming liquor brewed of herbs from Manfish Mountain, Witherwing spoke to Fish about the purpose of his sojourn with the snow-dwellers.

"Friend Fish, I have come to wish that the season of ice may never end and that we may never return to an earth where grass springs again. I have been born again in your house, and now I shall do what all must do when they are born—learn to live in the world. It is for this that Kryll has sent me to you, though I have no way to repay you for what is past, much less for what might come."

"Let's have no talk of payments," said Fish. "First, because Kryll will reward me richly enough, have no fear"—he shook with infectious laughter—"and, though you may not know how, you may well be serving Kryll's ends—whatever they may be, for I don't inquire."

Fish roared again in merriment at his splendid jokes, and Fox, Gull, Dog, Lizard and assorted animals echoed his mirth.

"And second," he continued, "you are a furnace to my house, which is hot with love and jollity. You are god's candle, and beyond price."

At which a strutting fowl jumped to the table round which they sat, defecated archly on the back of Fish's hand, and crowed as if cackling with laughter. Which was too much for the family, and mothers, children, dogs and fowls fell upon each other with gales of laughter. Some minutes later order reasserted itself.

"But yes," went on Fish, "you shall learn all that I can teach—how to build a house of snow, how to pluck fishes from the ice, and how to climb over the roof of the world. When you cross the mountains of ice, of course, there will be no fishing or hunting, for nothing lives there but wind and storm, but you will need to hunt again when you descend toward Karn-Ingli. To face thick ice and thin air takes courage and luck in the greatest measure, and those I need not or cannot teach you."

Fox, having licked her child, Dog, all over and replaced him in his warm bag of feathers, picked up her bone needle threaded with thin gut and said:

"Very soon I shall be ready with your clothes which, though you may walk like a duck, will keep you alive on the ice-peaks."

Surrounding her were new boots made of the thick water-proof hide of the snowbull with its abundant coarse hair as the lining, massive hooded coat and trousers of dense white fur, and undercoats of pale blue fish-skin. Dressed in these garments Witherwing and Nada spent the following days travelling with Fish, Gull and some of their village friends, a radiantly sensuous and crafty girl called Snake and a happy roistering giant aptly named Bear. They took two sleds and an indeterminate number of big dogs that lunged like panting foam over the snow. Supplies were bound upon the larger sled, which had runners longer than a man, each of which was fashioned out of a single unjointed piece of bone taken from the corpse of a blubberbeast that had been washed up on the snowcoasts a few years previously. The smaller sled ran on bones extracted from the grand architecture of the same skeleton, and its cradle, which accommodated two crouching bodies, was made from the complete rib-cages of two manfish. Jars of fish-oil were carried to provide light, but no fuel for cooking-fires was carried; any fresh meat caught was to be eaten raw.

On the first night they scooped out a hole in the frozen snow and covered it with skins held at the ends under ridges of impacted snow. Here all slept together without removing any of their clothes and, despite a desolate and cutting night wind which threw a hard white carpet over their roof, the atmosphere inside grew almost unbearably stuffy to Witherwing and Nada toward morning. Next day they descended, with the wind at their backs, to a small frozen lake which was said to feed Lizard Lake by a subterranean river. Through the morning they had crossed over a belt of soft snow which gave Witherwing and Nada the opportunity to walk with the oval frames woven with gut that formed a hitherto puzzling part of the tackle brought by Fish. The afternoon was well advanced by the time they reached the lake.

"Take one of these blades," said Fish to the prince, holding out to him a long and sharp-edged tongue of bone, "and watch. Snake and Bear will bring us windows and we shall build a house. Cut so."

Bear and Snake set off for the flat ice, playfully slapping each other's furclad rumps, and, when they came to a slope, rolling down together like puppies in a joyful yapping clinch.

Fish meanwhile made a neat vertical incision in the packed snow, then two others at the ends of the first. Along the fourth side he dug a trench and was so able to cut out a block of dressed snow, followed rapidly by another and another. Witherwing found it slow work when he applied himself, whereas Nada, though familiar only with the earthtents of her Flatland home, proved particularly adept at the block making and then in the construction of the round house which began to rise with remarkable speed under the hands and bone blade of Fish.

"You build him a fine house, lady," said the good-natured Fish. "Then you must fill it up with love fit to melt the walls away."

"I think I have lived too much with a cloak and a wing for a house," observed the prince, "to shine in these arts. But I think I could master a crooked kind of dwelling that would serve. And I welcome the melting of my walls by such love."

"See if we don't weary out our floor with it tonight," chuckled Fish, wrinkling his leather face in pleasure. "That too will be a lesson for survival in the snows."

"It's a bold time when snakes and bears entangle, that's for sure." Gull put in, pointing to where her friends were returning from the lake dragging on the sled three blocks of ice which were to be windows.

"I've set some lines," roared Bear. "So with luck we and the dogs can choke ourselves on fish tonight. Come down with me now, Prince Wing, and let me show you how it's done. And remember, mind you don't eat yellow snow!"

"Let's wait till we are ready here," said Fish, fitting a block of ice into the wall of snow that was gradually turning into a dome. When the top was finally finished Fish supervised the building of a long low tunnel as an entrance.

"To put some distance between us and the wind," he explained to Witherwing. "And to shelter the dogs, which makes it all the warmer for us."

"And makes for much-used air too," observed Witherwing.

"True, but it's warmer when it's used. Which is a proverb among our people."

Gull, Snake, and Bear all laughed appreciatively to indicate that they certainly intended to use it and keep warm.

"Come now, let's hear the lake speak and check the lines," said Fish.

So the whole group walked down and on to the ice together, pausing at the direction of Fish when they had left the shore a little way behind them. They stood in silence while the wind whipped powdery waves of snow around their ankles. After some moments there came from the further shore of the frozen lake a faint, almost musical groaning, something between a trumpet call and the falling of a gigantic tree, and once started the noise grew and spread at an alarming rate until it rumbled, raged and trumpeted beneath their feet as if the ice had cracked along a thousand veins. Witherwing felt that the lake must splinter and drown them, so overwhelming was the noise. But the roar sank to a grating sigh, and soon there was again no sound but the cruelly insistent lament of the wind across the unbroken surface of the lake.

"What does it mean that a lake should speak to us so?" asked Witherwing, who had arched his wing and tensed his feathers as the ice had fulminated at his feet.

"There are voices to all great things," said Fish. "Some say these voices are gods. And when you hear the great winds ringing out of the ice-peaks you might think so too."

"What gods are here?" inquired Witherwing.

"None, as you would know them," Fish answered. "The lake is a power, so is the mountain, so are the wind and snow . . ."

"The lake's power spoke to us," interjected Gull, "because we asked it to. The weight of all of us causes this floating sheet of ice to resettle itself. Those are Kryll's words."

"Ah, his lake booms like the earth's ready to split and spill itself out all over you," said Bear. "But let's look at the lines and set some more before it gets quite dark."

He took them to a hole that he had hacked in the thick ice, across which were laid two long bone spars with a strong line of gut descending into the dark water from the intersection. The line was still, so Bear led them toward his other fishing hole.

"Prince Wing," he said in a tone that suggested an anecdote was to follow, "I shall put another hole in the ice for you so you may see how it is done, but take warning from the tale of Rat, who was one of us and who, out of greed, surrounded himself with fishing holes on this lake and sat in the middle to await his first catch. But before that could happen the ice split from hole to hole and he found himself on a neat circle of an ice-floe that promptly tipped him into the water, righted itself and froze back over by morning. So we lost a Rat. Could that be him rattling to get out again after all these years?"

Sure enough there came a skeletal rattle from somewhere ahead of them.

"Fish for all, I think," said Snake as she and the others saw that it was the crossed bones over the second ice-hole that were being agitated from below. At the same time Snake turned her sly eyes up to Fish with a knowing and seductive look, which set them all laughing again.

"I've heard that snakes will drop their skins with ease," said Fish in the same spirit.

"And I have heard that when you go groping after trout they are to be had for the tickling," said Snake, capping him.

"Believe me, such a tickler is not to be found every day," bellowed Bear. Then he pointed to the ice-hole and the straining line. "But let's raise this fellow before we start raising any others. I feel like tickling my throat with some slabs of sweet fish meat."

Snake smirked round the company till all burst into a fresh storm of laughter while Bear rolled about the ice clutching his sides and shouting:

"Damn, thunder, damn! What things she makes me say! I take the very words from her mouth!"

It was some ten minutes before order was restored and Bear began to haul in the line which by now was stirring only weakly as the snared fish became exhausted. Bear gave a shout of triumph as a large scaled white head with bulbous eyes broke the surface, followed by a long fat body and a gleaming tail which thrashed up a silvery foam of fury with its last reserves of strength. Standing back to admire his catch, Bear allowed the fish to flap its bulk ineffectually on the ice and snap its ugly jaws at nothing. Then he killed and gutted the fish, docking its head and tail—which, together with some more palatable fragments, were thrown to the excited dogs—and dripping uncooked fish steaks were soon in everybody's hands and mouths. Witherwing and Nada found that if they chewed small amounts of flesh for a long time it became pleasant as well as nourishing, but their friends bolted their food almost without chewing and, more surprisingly, without choking, though they belched with relish as, after the first onslaught of self-cramming, they fed each other teasingly with choice titbits. They continued this playful meal until the fish was wholly devoured even though another catch announced itself at the first ice-hole, but when it was over they grouped themselves about the potential new meal, and Bear asked if Witherwing would like to try his hand—and his wing—at this one. In fact, the wing proved an obstacle to the operation, for though he could raise the fish easily enough with his hand without being distracted by the thrashing struggle, he had difficulty in holding it with the wing ready for the knife in the gills. When eventually he seemed to have overcome the problem Bear called out to him:

"You're holding him over the hole! If he slips we'll lose him. Just move him away before you put the knife in."

But before Witherwing could do anything the ice-hole bubbled, boiled, and burst, and a large blue head shot like a column into the air, then slipped the dark glove of its mouth round the hooked fish and, like a piston-stroke, shot back into the foaming water.

"Manfish!" exclaimed Bear. "Good thing he hadn't swallowed before we pulled in."

The snowdwellers were strangely serious about this occurrence. The loss of a fish did not seem to Witherwing to merit great concern, especially when most of them had feasted so substantially already. Since he was here to learn, he asked about it:

"True, I was surprised to see the manfish, but I don't sense we've been endangered by his intrusion. Yet he seems to have robbed you of your humor. There are, I presume, other fish to be caught—so why this anxiety?"

Gull, who appeared to be the most analytic of the group, answered thoughtfully.

"This is difficult to answer, for we do not fear attack from the manfish. But he brings a chill to us, not as severe and deadly as the furbeast, but it is of that kind. The manfish, like the lake, is a power, and his power is the causing of fright."

This was all he could elicit, and it was a muted group that turned back in the dusk toward the snowhouse. But Witherwing was sure that the depression would not last long, though he had begun to realize that beneath the dog-like lust for life of these affectionate people there was a fixed and permanent layer of fear and unknowing such as he had encountered through all the world that he had yet seen. Once again he had witnessed the merest crack in a door that opened on to dread and emptiness.

During the night they piled their all against that door with hectic naked romps in the fur-piled snowhouse that flared, died down, flared again, and again, and so on till their small dome of snow, its entrance plugged by a river of furry dogs, held air so thick and hot that Witherwing and Nada woke giddy before dawn. Fish, Snake, Bear, and Gull were all pleased with each other in various combinations at various times, and Snake went so far as to stroke her sweat-gold breasts upon the prince's out-stretched wing before he slept. Later he woke from a pleasant dream to find in his lap Snake's insinuating soft-lipped head, and he did not trouble to disturb her; nor did he trouble, on the next day, to ask Nada if she had received any comparable visitation in her sleep. These were unacknowledged courtesies that could pass, if one wished, for dreams, and on the following night Witherwing dreamed, very vividly, that he woke to find his lips on the wing-enfolded grace of Nada's brown body while Gull's head was where Snake's had been.

On the third day Fish led his party across the lake in search of what his people called simply The Bay, because the sea came within range of their travel at no other point. This tongue of salt water was so long and narrow that it could almost pass for an inland lake, and in the cold season it gradually froze into a heaped-up jagged surface that extended a morning's travel before meeting the heaving floe-filled border of dark salt waves. As they dropped down toward The Bay, Witherwing's education continued: they endured a sudden storm which buried them and their tents in deep snow before it abated; they lost a dog down a crevasse, and rescued another by lowering Fish to him; they scaled and descended icy rock faces using harnesses of gut and rope for themselves and the dogs. On a windless day during a thick and silent fall of snow they came suddenly to the sea.

As best they could in such conditions, they set up their tents on the featureless shore and huddled inside while snow piled thickly over them. The dogs just lay down outside and allowed themselves to be buried. Bear told some fishing stories of increasingly dubious veracity before drowsiness spread over them like snow and all dozed in a warm huddle waiting for the sky to clear, so that, if the light lasted, they could shape a better-appointed camp.

Witherwing woke with a start he did not know how much later, and the feeling of something wrong was on him, perhaps, he thought at first, persisting from a troubled dream caused by the considerable stuffiness of this place. But there was no mistaking the sound of alien voices outside carried down through the muffling snow. Witherwing had no way to judge how far the speakers might be from where he lay—possibly they were standing over him now, discussing the significance of this mound of snow—so he waited a while, knife in hand, and when it seemed that the voices had receded he carefully burrowed through the snow, breaking a hole in the crust, to which he could set his eyes. It was still snowing, but more thinly now, and in the increased visibility he could see that the shore was broken by many mounds, ridges, and depressions, so that their own camp, as long as it remained still, would be safe from discovery. Which was well for Witherwing and his friends, for moving along the skirt of the sea, where waves turned into rough sharp fingers of ice, were the dim gray shapes of a dozen or so men that looked like ghosts—especially the tall figure who brought up the rear, for on his head he bore a pair of massive branching horns.

Witherwing slid silently through to the surface, uncovered the larger sled, and took from it a short and vicious spear; he would have preferred to have been able to use one of the powerful rib-bone bows that were there, but with his wing he could not handle these. Crouching hunter-fashion he began to shadow Hrasp and his warriors with a firmness and concentration frightening in their intensity. All his

fury at the killer of Hutt and the raider of the Flatlands was bound by an iron purpose, and every
movement he made was sure and implacable; he
felt he was like a poisoned arrow in flight.

Shortly the group that Witherwing followed
joined with more gray figures who were engaged on
some task by the sea's ice-wrinkled edge. Shouts suggestive of strenuous activity mingled with the greetings, and the newcomers appeared to go immediately
to the assistance of the five or six men whom they
met. The snow had almost stopped now, but Witherwing was able to approach fairly close under cover of
a slight rise in the snow without being observed by
Hrasp's men, who were intent upon their own business. He saw that they stood more or less in a line
straining upon a taut rope that stretched into the
choppy water slapping upon the ice. Hrasp-the-Hunter was at the back, pulling mightily and shouting
curses of encouragement, which soon had their effect as a contorted blue head was dragged at the end
of the line from the water on to the cruel frag-
mented ice. The blue head screamed like a man,
which caused Witherwing to shudder, and he knew
that he was witnessing the taking of a manfish.
Some of the dread of his snowdwelling friends stole
over him as the terrified screams continued and the
blue body was hauled on the ripping shore. Witherwing had expected to see short flapping fins at the
side of the manfish, and, indeed, the creature was
finned, but these were not fish-like, they were
more like a man's arms, and webbed fingers grabbed
like a man at jutting slabs of ice in a desperate and
hopeless attempt to resist the pull of the Karns.
The small back finned feet of the manfish tore a trail
across the ice as they scrambled for a firmer grip.
Most horrible was the face of the manfish, its eyes

rolling and its bleeding mouth wrenched out of shape by the line it had swallowed; for this was not a face like that of the glum white fish that Witherwing had seen hooked back at the lake—it was a man's face, and it expressed a man's feelings. Witherwing, who had loved a Snakeskin woman, caught the reek of deep blasphemy from the scene.

The manfish, now well clear of the water, tried to raise itself on its arm-fins, but as it did so four Karns let go of the rope and began to beat the creature's head with clubs of heavy bone. Still the manfish struggled, waving its crushed head from side to side, uttering a low groaning hoot of the deepest misery. Tears gushed from its eyes and rolled down the bleeding face.

Hrasp-the-Hunter approached the fading animal, rammed an antler under its upturned head and jabbed a knife into the soft exposed throat, continuing the thrust of his blade right down the body so he could take the skin off like a coat—which he did, while the manfish still heaved and quivered on the reddened snow.

Witherwing had looked on many scenes of cruelty, had killed both animals and men, but the pure horror of the manfish killing rendered him senseless.

When he recovered he rose and gripped his spear with steadiness, his deadly gaze all filled with the antlered giant strutting in triumph over his red trophy. The spear was raised, but never thrown, for a restraining hand was laid upon the prince, who turned to see sad-eyed Fish behind him and, a few paces further off, Nada.

"Now you know. But your time for Hrasp is not yet come. They are too many."

Witherwing lowered his spear, and they slipped away while Hrasp sliced up his unholy feast.

15

*King Rumi, Lord of Tum-Barlum, to his scribe, the
fiftieth day since Leaf-fall in Lizard-year:*

"I am become a hollow king; robes, crown, and
throne mask only a mind that is like mist on the sea.
Harand and Ring are dead, and I know their deaths
to have been ignoble as I know they were bound to
evil and ignoble courses. On all sides things fall
away from us without remedy or purpose. There are
no grand destinies for kingdoms in this world, for
nothing here replenishes itself faster than it dies. I
am Lord of a shrinking kingdom and barren as a
rock. My sons die and are not replaced. Our short
history is no more than a tale, our future even less.
Being king, I have seen through to the world of
those who control, and that too is barren and deadly
and disengaged from us. We have no appeals, and
we are not cared for, and there is nothing at the
heart of life. I was wedded to a pale witch who
showed me death and terror in a box of stones. She
spoke with bodiless powers, sent her words into the
empty air and from it plucked back answers—all
amounting to nothing, except a little more death.
Many years I fretted to discover her purpose: now
I think it was nothing, that she had none, that it

was less than dream or play to her. Yet we have put it at the center of our lives, and our bards have made it something shapely. In truth the center of our lives is a black hole that devours the universe. I cloak it from my people with a king's robe, a feast, and a fire.

"The Forest Folk have brought me news also of Witherwing, who has passed the black tower of Kryll, and has done well according to our codes—which is of some value. But too many here despise him secretly for a mutation, as did his brother Harand—I cannot mourn his death, for he would have made a bloody king. His were the plans to keep the Snakeskins in pens and so exterminate them all; he even had some built, but now he has paid for his fanatic viciousness. He also pressed most hard to send his youngest brother on the quest for power from the Upper Lands—power for himself as king, or the removal of a mutant brother, either way he won according to his lights. I fear that Witherwing will find a deathly power, if anything, and cannot wish it brought back to my land. Yet Harand was but one of many who lusted when rumor came of power to be won—no more than evil whispers, and when we above all have reason to shun whatever's touched by that white witch of dread . . . I, most surely, who have known her coiled embraces . . . But my son may acquire merit in his own eyes before death—I wish him that. I think I shall not see him again. I have my duty in a fading world, though death swills in me like water in a cave."

The tongueless scribe offers the silence of death if he break silence in life.

Rookery-high through the giant trees swung the spidery branch-like form of the messenger of the Forest

151

Folk returning from Rumi's High Hall, where he had been regarded with deep suspicion and even open hostility by all but the king himself. Pausing on a thick and sinuous branch, where his profile showed like a smaller tree growing in the larger, he thrust his twig-like fingers into the breast of his dark garment and brought out a placid white bird, to whose foot he attacked a small twist of bark parchment beaten thin. There was a rattle of twigs as he tossed the bird up into the air where it wheeled higher and higher, then sped off in the direction of the flatlands.

Like a fall of angel-snow white birds clustered on the pointed roof of Kryll's black tower.

16

"My earliest memories," said Nada, "are of my people in flight from the Horde which for three years devoured the Flatlands. At twelve years I was raped and left for dead by four of Hrasp's slaves who killed my elder brother. In the next year I went to live in the earthtent of my cousin and bore his still-born child; this cousin was killed by Hrasp. And this year Hutt has followed him. By which I mean to tell you two things: First, that I will take an equal share with you in all your movements against Hrasp, including the fighting, for I have strength of arm as well as the sense to put a dagger in the back when the chance is given me. Second, that I do not have false hopes that anything will last. I have been a survivor and have learned that lesson well."

The freckled hollow of her cheek and her dark eye had held from the first a beauty of tragic intensity for Witherwing. Even a prince with a magic wing could not meet her as less than his equal; he could not protect her from what she had endured already, he could not spin a fiction that warriors suffer for a woman's comfort, nor did he wish to make her some flimsy confection of romance.

"I understand," he replied; "though I did not

gain such understanding from girls in my own land. I knew a Snakeskin woman through whom I saw these things; but I had too short a time to learn— now I have a new life to set against the deaths I have found." He paused, allowing a picture of the past to form; then he continued reflectively. "I too remember the Horde, though it never smothered Tum-Barlum as it did the Flatlands. We made warriors out of boys to prod that monster from our borders. I was one such in the last year when it rolled back. Flatlanders sheltered in our valleys, but I don't think we made them welcome."

Witherwing recalled the black sea against which Harand had uselessly pitted his men, the scything and the waves of blood, the gray rain which had wrapped him around and entered his heart. He remembered falling into the void of that sea, the naked struggle for life in the midst of chaos and, at last, the detached logic which had saved him from the whirlpool. He remembered the ring of fire and the still-falling rain which had turned a boy's naked body to gold. Perhaps at that time the child Nada had been hiding in the unwelcoming hills into which he had helped to channel the Horde and, now grown, had reached into him and drawn aside the gray curtain at his heart.

Nada and Witherwing lay curled in a snowhouse of their own making as they recalled the way in which the Horde had touched their lives. It was several days now since they had trod over the roofs of Fish's people and set out up the pass which took them above the line at which snow never melted. They had a foot upon the ramparts of the world, to which the mountains they had passed before were merely piles of rubble shaken carelessly from the knees of the ice-peaks, and with each ascent new changeless heights revealed themselves beyond. A day of walking in these chill and lordly mountains seemed no advance at all, inducing a mood of dream-like suspension which would have been consistently frustrating had it not been for the inconceivable vastness of the peak world. Sometimes they would look down at a small distant turbulence in a mighty white ocean and realize that they were witnessing a storm that could create a toppling avalanche to smother Manfish Mountain; and when such a storm engulfed them they were fully aware of the likelihood that it would bury them so deep that a new mountain of snow might serve as their grave monument. They saw whirling white columns meandering through valleys of ice, looking like peaceful white ghosts, but they knew that if one of these winds came near them they would be snatched up defenseless into the roaring vortex. Once, after a weary day's travel up a seemingly endless desert of snow, they set up camp to find in the morning that they had slept on an overhanging lip of snow that looked down on a stupendous precipice whose silent depths could only be guessed at, since far below lay a shroud of mist which never cleared. They would set their course for a mere ripple, which would at last become an enormous green-shadowed wall of ice, and when it had shrunk again to a small fold in the landscape the white thumbnail they had made for next had grown into a huge lake of snow, and there was still no perceptible change in the relative positions of those distant gods among mountains which it would be death to scale.

Sometimes they themselves felt like gods as, with one sweep of the eye, they saw black clouds tiny with distance grumble thunder at a mountaintop, great winds dancing with its snowy skirt, and endless rigid peaks like waves outlined with fire toward sunset. At other times they felt like two fleas upon an iceberg in an empty ocean.

They encountered no animals in these regions, but the cold was like a beast which could not be shaken off while the thin air slowed them. Their lips turned white and cracked and when licked they were coated at once with ice. Witherwing's beard bore a constant frost and the hairs in their nostrils were frozen stiff. Their faces, where exposed, suffered greatly with the skin turning hard and brown and splitting, while their eyes narrowed into slits like those of the villagers of the pass that led to the eternal snows. When caught in a bitter wind Witherwing and Nada would have the terrifying conviction that their eyeballs were about to turn to ice. It was with dread that they numbly removed a glove or hood when they sheltered, fearing that they might find a finger or ear snapped off, as Fish had warned could happen.

Permanent changes were being wrought upon their bodies by ice, storm and sun, which planted seeds of pains and twinges that would never be uprooted, and hunger attacked them from within. But the prince and the Flatland girl had found much to endure in life before they entered the ice-peaks, and they endured now. Neither set great store by the notion that only the unused can be beautiful, so there was no sentimental regret at the way the frozen world assailed them.

In the uncertain flicker of a fish-oil taper Witherwing looked with love into Nada's brown face.

"Nada, we have come crawling like flies up over the spine of the world, which few enough have done before—and fewer still have lived to tell of it—and even when you fled from the Horde into the swamplands you cannot have known a harder life than this."

"Nor a more magnificent," she reminded him. "This is surely no place for men, but great daring brings its own reward, and to have been here is a worthy growth."

"I feel this too. Otherwise it would pain me to have brought you here when my aims are so uncertain," said Witherwing. "There is vengeance on Hrasp-the-Hunter, which I shall take if I can, though I don't lust for blood for its own sake. I could have waited for him on the Flatland borders, but I have been strangely drawn to these mountains, to see Karn-Ingli beyond them, and take Hrasp on his own ground. The quest for which I left Tum-Barlum is more obscure, but something waits for me in the Upper Lands that is beyond and above Hrasp—Kryll confirms this, though it is hard to know his meanings exactly."

"He would have held us from this journey if this were not true," said Nada. "Instead he gave us direct encouragement by his help. Fish says—and I think it's right—that we serve Kryll's ends as much as our own."

"I can't think what his ends might be. For myself, I have some mysteries, some dreams that have haunted me, which might be explained should I discover the secrets of the Queen of Dread who stole me and my brothers from Tum-Barlum and, so the story goes, made swans of us. Kryll spoke cryptically on these matters, but I think it's his belief that if explanations are to be had at all they are by definition worthless."

"This Queen—she is the one of whom you dreamed when the furbeast attacked before the death of Hutt?"

Witherwing shuddered.

"That was like no dream I've known before, and since I was a child I've dreamed of her. The furbeast is a terror and a mystery to me that is somehow connected with that pale witch. And the manfish haunts me too, for when he looked up at me, dying, his eyes . . ."

"I know," said Nada, "I saw it too. It was as if Hutt looked out at us. I don't know what it means."

"Do you think that you may find an answer in the Upper Lands?"

"It was Hutt who called me to you, and he knew where you were bound and that he would die. What his thoughts were, whether he had ends in mind, no one could tell, but it is certain that when he brought about an action it was never without result—you, who have been saved by him more than once, will know that."

"He was deep as Kryll, and even more inscrutable."

"Kryll thinks that you are seeking out your death."

"Nada, this is not true. It may be that the power of the glowing stones, for which I was sent to search, are the seeds of death, and we should have little reason to desire them in Tum-Barlum again seeing who brought them before. The kingdom wants the power without the dread, and I have doubted since before ever meeting Kryll that this is possible. But I want to confront the Queen of Dread, because I want to *know*—about my people and their history, and why she came to us, about myself. Ignorance is like death to me. Not just our own lives, but the lives of our whole people is a mere flutter of a bird's wing. Kryll has shown me bottomless pits. I even entered one, and now I am at the roof of the world.

"No, I am less concerned with death than most in this world. Think how many sayings of your people are of death, and it is the same with mine. How much does your tribe grow every year?"

"I think it hardly grows at all," answered Nada.

"So it is in Tum-Barlum. Beware of the time when Hrasp-the-Hunter no longer pillages your earth-tents, when you are no longer worth it. For then you will be like Fish's people, on the brink of extinction. And I fear this will happen to the Flatlands, to Tum-Barlum, to the Snakeskins, Yellowmanes, and Forest-Folk as it has to others before."

And with that thought Witherwing and Nada, fighting against the cold, tried to sleep.

Life beneath the snow in the house of Fish had been an idyll of love, almost languorous, whereas now the lovers were engaged in a fierce and wasting battle for existence. The great consolation for all the rigors endured was that they were not drawn apart by selfishness or by impatience with each other. Their love enriched itself through hardship; like the air it grew more rarefied, like their bodies it acquired a lasting sinewy strength even as it shed itself of sleekness.

One day, as Witherwing and Nada toiled up a breast of snow that bolstered a cloud-capped icepeak, they saw, faint and far, a slim shaft of smoke rise where the landscape lay clear.

On another day Witherwing learned to fly.

Though they journeyed always in the shadow of the lordly mountains whose immense meadows of ice had never felt a foot, for no creature could have breathed at such heights, the travellers scaled hills that had seemed unimaginably lofty to them. The tallest peaks stood in the same relation to Witherwing and Nada as the moon, but they were as often dizzied by looking down as up. Witherwing had looked down one morning and the snow he stood on turned to powder and emptied him over a precipice. Round him tumbled a white and rushing world, the gray dome of the sky twisted over him, and a flashing vista of far mountains, and Withering thought of Kryll.

"I am falling," he thought. "This is dying."

He seemed to be falling from the sky into the sky, for the valley below was filled with the same gray cloud as was overhead. A wind swept up at the prince, snatching the heavy green cloak which he still wore over the clothes given to him by Fish and his family, so that he seemed suspended by the neck from a thick green rope—which was not far from the truth as his flying garment began to choke him and the wind became a wall of solid cold that could not be swallowed. Then his swan's wing was ripped into that cold rush. He was jolted and rolled over, but his fall ceased to accelerate at the same disastrous rate, and just as he was about to lose consciousness Witherwing spread his feathers as in a painful dream. For a moment he floated on a cold but reviving cushion of air before going into a spin which caused him to fall again, faster and faster, as the wind seemed intent on plucking his wing feather by streaming feather.

But Witherwing had done it once, so now he made the effort to spread again his wing against the upward-slamming air. At first he jutted it out short and falcon-like, maneuvering himself into a position as if hanging from the branch of a tree by fanning the strong feathers on the outer trailing edge of his wing, after which he thrust out more of his secondary feathers on the inner edge to give greater lift or resistance. How he longed for a body covered in close-meshed feathers against the cold of the gust on which he now almost rode! With his right arm Witherwing succeeded in grasping his outflung cloak which, though it could not be controlled like a wing, provided a steadying wind resistance, so that soon, with strong paddling motion made by his wing, he was able to shift his body from hanging in the air to lying spreadeagled upon it. Numb-faced he spiralled down, barely able to glimpse the snowfast landscape around him or the piled mist below. After a while it seemed that this falling flight would never end, and the prince began to hear a high and glorious singing in which blood and wind made up the choir. He still thought he would die, but now he felt it with a sense of triumph, as if somehow he had come into his own.

Suddenly he dropped into the mist. Ground and sky were hidden from him, and he could not tell whether or not he still descended, for he had lost all feeling. Without knowing why he gave a count of two and then threw up his arm and wing, so that he fell feet first, air swirling by the opened vanes of the wing, and straight away he plunged through a hard crust of snow. He was not dead, or even damaged, only breathless and in a strange lazy daze.

It was as if he had drunk an impossible liquor distilled from flowers of diamond ice on the summits of the highest mountains in the world; and the intoxication lasted dangerously long, for if a warm sleep were to come upon him exposed in this way he would already have acquiesced to death. But at last he rose to take his bearings, only to find that there was nothing to take them from—snow at his feet and mist all around him. Darkness would fall much quicker in the deep valleys than on the eminence from which he had drifted. He wanted to make his way to the end of the valley and from there repeat the previous day's journey till he had climbed to the camp where he had left Nada; but he could not tell which way the valley ran. He was about to set out in a direction chosen at random, just hoping that he would not walk in circles, when he remembered Kryll's needle, the magic finger that would point him to Karn-Ingli. The valley into which he had fallen was, as far as he could recall, more or less straight and running in the direction of Hrasp's cloudy kingdom. The sharp end of the needle, then, should point toward the upper reach of the valley and all Witherwing needed to do was to follow where the blunt end directed, turning squarely to the left after what seemed a sufficient distance and so rise above the cloud up the valley's flank, which was the lower part of the ridge from which he had fall-en. "Had flown," he corrected himself as these thoughts went through his mind.

He reached Nada and the camp again just as he had planned. Except that he was nearly dead through exposure when he arrived.

He had stumbled back after a shivering sleepless night in such a shelter as he was able to make when tired and ill-equipped. The frost had nibbled at his face, and as he fell into Nada's arms his ravaged lips moved for a few moments before he fainted and he said:

"Did you think . . . I'd flown away?"

17

For some days after his flight Witherwing rested
in a dark huddle with Nada, feeding on strips of
cured meat and chewing more or less constantly on
a strong-tasting restorative root provided by Fish. At
first both felt that they might never move from the
spot, though neither of them mentioned the possibility, and it is likely that they were not inwardly
daunted by it. They were not tempted to let go, simply to allow death to float them away, but certainly
there were many less palatable ways of dying. Of
course, it was impossible to be comfortable on this
journey—the cold could never be forgotten; the thin
air and the vastness of the snowy waste sapped the
strength; the lovers could find warmth in each other's
arms, but their garments were bulky and awkward,
their bodies subject to cramps and numbness. But
even during the prince's weakness they experienced
also the elation of survivors; they almost came to
believe consciously that this was their special destiny—to survive. The discomfort of their situation was
inseparable from its sublimity. In this world it was
fitting that one might fly and equally fitting that he
be brought to the edge of death in so doing.

So they survived, and, digging themselves out

of what had seemed set to become a tomb in the snow, faced again the cold rolling air of the mountains. Once, still far from them, they saw smoke again, and then, when their minds had become mesmerized and blinded like their snow-tired eyes, so that it seemed to them that they had always been in the mountains and always would be, they began to descend. At first they did not notice, because right across the ice-peaks they had been ascending and descending, but there came a time when they were aware that they had been coming down for longer than ever before, that their lungs felt fuller, that their legs had found a new energy. In fact, they lost the nightmarish impression of endless effort and motion in which no progress could ever be made. Hills still lay before them, but the towering lords of the earth were behind. Time began to have some meaning again and the sense of space ceased to reduce their bodies to virtually nothing. It seemed too that they had left behind the storms of such ruinous violence in which whole mountains appeared to burst apart as if the earth were inflicting mortal wounds upon itself.

Over the distant horizon toward which Nada and the prince were making hung a constant mass of cloud, a billowing forest of ivory vapor, of the sort which tells seafarers that they are approaching an island, and once or twice they fancied that a warm breeze blew out to them from that quarter. When they dropped down to a frozen lake in the lower hills the impression of a rise in temperature appeared contradicted, for though they attacked the ice with all possible vigor they were unable to break through and set fishing lines. But after a day-long slithering descent down a defile that sported magnificent humped and streaming growths of green ice—

showing that they were now out of the eternal snows, for this was where the lake emptied itself in warmer seasons—they came to another valley basin where a lake had formed. By now it was evident that beneath the great swathe of snow lay vegetation, and the tops of pine trees pushed up small pyramids on the surface. Here the snow was softer and often more difficult to negotiate, so that more than once they were swallowed in tree-high drifts, but on the ice they were able to hack through to the dark water, from which they soon plucked a number of sweet silver fish.

"Brother fish," said Witherwing in a Kryll-like tone as he hauled in his fourth wriggling catch and held it before his face, "forgive my intrusion, but do me the honor of coalescing with me and we shall see some interesting sights together. Your namesake has sent me to meet you. He's quite well, as is his family. And now let's eat."

"I wonder if that's how Hrasp talks to his man-fish," mused Nada.

Witherwing's face clouded at the recollection of that vicious scene which, though in some way everything in his life before his experience in the ice-peaks had grown more distant, estranged and dreamlike, still brought rage and terror bubbling within him.

"If Kryll is right," went on Nada, "there cannot be much difference between his slaughter of the man-fish and what we are doing now."

"Do you believe this?"

"No. But they need the manfish for food, skin and oil, just as we need fresh food now. And they had to fight for it; perhaps, then, they deserve the fruits of struggle."

"This would seem reasonable if I did not remember that killing so well," said Witherwing. "But what they did was like a cruel self-disembowelling, full of bitterness. They were raging for extinction, not pursuing life. They looked as if they were trying to drag the deepest life-blood out of themselves."

"They hate themselves, and they hate life."

"And Kryll—do you think it doesn't matter to him that they kill his lizards? I wear a coat of liazard-mail, and I have seen Kryll throw one of his lizards down to death; but he didn't do that out of hatred, it was out of a desperate kind of love—and if he can love those lizards, he's really achieved something. Hrasp-the-Hunter deserves to be stuck underground with them for ever—there would be plenty of scope for self-despising there."

"These are good answers," said Nada. "When appetite and reverence are the same there's perfect balance."

"And when we've finished eating these fish I shall start on you, and do that with appetite and reverence too," laughed Witherwing, flapping his swan's wing in an expansive gesture as if it were a flag signalling the return of strength.

That night they camped at the foot of the ice-falls behind an intricately sculpted curtain of trans-lucent green and blue ice that, when the dawn came up, splashed its jewelled radiance over them. As they lay gazing at the play of sun through the thick-ribbed ice a shadow rippled across the surface, and in the sudden breathless silence on their side of the bright wall Witherwing and Nada heard from the other the sounds of feet crunching in the snow and of breath-ing that came in unpleasant snuffles and snorts. At first it was impossible to deduce the shape of the creature from the constantly shifting patches and shafts of darkness that moved over the ice like a splintered reflection in agitated water; but gradually, as it passed back and forth, Witherwing deciphered from the shadow the slovenly loose-limbed gait which induced in him a sick dread. With Nada he had survived the eternal snows—only to be found out now by a furbeast.

He motioned to Nada that she should remain silent and still, and then he slid out his blade from the rib-cage sled next to where they lay and, without donning his heavy fur over-garment, picked his way toward the opening where they had entered the ice-cave on the previous night. It did not seem possible that he could overcome the furbeast without Hutt, for no reliance could be placed on the sword or on physical courage, and the prince could remember all too well the smothering nightmare with which his mind had been blanketed on the first occasion that the furbeast had slammed into him. However, he hoped that by going out to meet the creature he might keep it from Nada; perhaps he could even surprise it, though this seemed unlikely, since the furbeast possessed, albeit in a degraded form, something like the mind-power of Hutt.

At the cave opening Witherwing turned to Nada and mouthed silently:

"Don't move. Not at all."

For this encounter his mind must be nerved as much as his arm; this knowledge gave him an advantage which had not been his at the last terrifying assault—for what it was worth. So he clamped his inner vision upon the image of Kryll's bottomless well with steel determination, seeing fathoms down the agonized stretched face of the manfish at the end of a line which, at the rim of the pit, Hrasp-the-

Hunter hauled upward. Witherwing encompassed this image with words he repeated like a charm inwardly:

"I can face it. I can do it."

And all his energy and resolution gathered in his sword which glowed with the power and which was poised to slice through the line on which Hrasp was exerting his giant's strength.

This imagined picture was Witherwing's fortress against the furbeast, and it did not take away from his concentration on his present physical circumstances. Flat as a lizard he peered from the cave, showing little more than a narrowed eye, and he noted with grim satisfaction that there had been snow in the night to obliterate the tracks of yesterday. There was a slight hope, then, that the furbeast was unaware of their presence. The drooping shaggy animal was moving away from him along the back of the ice-wall, sniffing like an idiot and occasionally scratching between its legs then staring slack-jawed at its hands with all the appearance of mental vacancy. Without paying any attention to it at all the furbeast urinated in the snow, broke wind, scratched himself some more, was about to shuffle on when it stopped with a sudden alertness ...

Witherwing knew what would follow; he felt the nightmare reaching out for his mind with strangling tentacles. Furiously he concentrated on the image of Kryll's well, the manfish, and Hrasp, forcing it to stretch right across his thought, to repel any intrusion. His outer eye was fixed upon the motionless furbeast, his inner upon Hrasp's taut fishing line and upon his own power-humming sword.

"Face it. Do it."

A great surge through his arm—a fleshing electric arc as his blade swings down upon the line and cleaves it clean through—the manfish sinking free—Hrasp-the-Hunter facing the surge and spread of an opened swan's wing that like some cleansing cloth wipes out the antlered giant along with Kryll's cellar and his pit, leaving . . . nothing.

The furbeast continued to snuffle desultorily around the urine-pitted snow, then wandered off with his awkward droop toward the lake, where he stood like an oaf.

Witherwing, who had watched all this as if his eyes were on other scenes, became all at once conscious of the sword gripped so tight in his hand that it quivered as in his vision. A wave of compassion for the drooling man-parody swelled from his heart, and quietly he lay down his sword.

"That I should kill this . . . thing . . . this *man-thing* . . ."

He watched the furbeast shuffle around the frozen ice till it came to Witherwing's fishing hole, now skinned with ice again. Down on his haunches went the furbeast, lolling his head into the hole, poking at it with one arm. Then a dark matted leg tried the ice and went through, causing the whole body to tumble splashing out of sight. It rose again suddenly, an acid gout spewed up from the lake's belly. There was a scrambling of paws—or hands—on the side of the ice-pit, a scraping and breaking of claws that scored frosty grooves down to the water itself. Briefly the water boiled, then was still as if sealed over, and slowly ice began to form again over that small hole.

As they neared the mass of cloud, Witherwing and Nada passed through frozen forests rather than over them. This was no longer an empty world, for now they often heard the whooping of the snowbird and sometimes caught a glimpse of its flashing white wings and the orange glare of its eyes as it fled from them. By digging up dead wood from under the snow and using their last stocks of oil it even became possible for them to have a fire again, which was a laborious task, but worth it to them after their long deprivation. They hunted a tree-climbing pigrat of a kind unfamiliar to them; roasted, it was luxury unbounded to them in comparison with the supplies that had served them through the ice-peaks. The quickening of life around them was heavy with warning too, and it was not long before they came across the recent tracks of a large sled drawn by a correspondingly large snowbull. They grew accustomed to seeing columns of smoke from camp fires to which they gave a wide berth. When they came to a flat open stretch of country where a sizeable herd of high-legged horned swine rooted about through the snow, they assumed that these were wild animals, but—luckily before they had ventured far from the cover of the woods—it became clear that they were being tended and fed by Karns, who moved among them in their distinctive white fur and blue manfish skin.

The prince considered killing some of the Karns and disguising himself and Nada in their clothes so as to enter Karn-Ingli unnoticed, but he rejected this course, partly because of the difficulty of concealing his wing, because neither he nor Nada had anything like the coloring of the yellow-haired Karns and because, as far as he could tell, the land would afford them adequate shelter to bring them close to the heart of Hrasp's kingdom. If he started killing now it would probably serve only to announce his arrival, which would defeat in advance the object of disguise. Obviously he was expected—before he had even reached Kryll's tower efforts had been made to stop him. After meeting Kryll, despite the killing of Hutt by Hrasp's own hand, he himself had not been molested again, which suggested a mystery Witherwing would not penetrate. Presumably Hrasp could have killed him instead of Hutt—or would Hutt have stopped him? Witherwing hoped that Hrasp was assuming that the journey through the eternal snows would prove impossible for him without the boy's power of mind, but he was hardly confident in this hope.

By now the temperature, though cold, had perceptibly risen so that Witherwing reverted to his Tum-Barlum clothes, which allowed him much greater freedom of movement and were more suited to his present purpose, which demanded not slow endurance, but quickness, cunning, and violence. The ground itself seemed warmer, and they came upon rocky patches quite bare of snow and later upon a gash in the earth's skin from which rose hissing steam, melting the snow and uncovering brown soil for some distance around. These fissures grew larger and more frequent as they progressed, developing at some points into thick dark ponds which heaved and bubbled, throwing up an acrid yellow steam, and along the verges of the more extensive of these hot cracks lay almost unmoving piles of mud-colored snakes with eyes like stones. Witherwing wondered what they ate—each other, or even themselves, he thought, remembering his subterranean view of Kryll's lizards. Anyway he avoided them, and when he saw one of the snakes raise its dull head with astonishing whiplike rapidity and snatch in its jaws a snowbird that had skimmed too low, he knew that his care was justified. There were still enough available pigrats to keep Witherwing from sampling the snakes as food, and, from the size of the swellings he sometimes saw in the snakes bellies, he imagined that they liked to partake of the passing pigrat too. He saw on one occasion a pool of hot mud bubble with an unusually large quantity of steaming gas which sent a dark tongue flopping out over the edge to lick up and fry the snakes who basked there; almost as soon as the mud had settled or run back into the pool, the snakes that had survived pushed the frazzled corpses into the mud and moved in more closely round the heat.

Witherwing and Nada could build fires with complete safety now, since amid all this steam and smoke one more wisp would pass unnoticed; but there was no longer any need for fire, as they could rest warmly by a snake-free steaming rift and boil the pigrat flesh there too.

They had entered a long cloudy valley which was the land of Karn-Ingli, and the valley floor eventually turned into a recognizably beaten track. When they came to a pair of rudely carved wooden stakes, planted on each side of the road, at the top of which were sets of huge branching antlers and a ring of lizard skulls, Witherwing and Nada knew that it was time to skirt the road. So they took to the slopes where at first there were only a few outlying hovels to be avoided, turf and timber shacks dug into the side of the valley, and even if the inhabitants had seen them—which was far from certain—they did not have the appearance of eager informers; rather they had a mole-like air of wishing not to be disturbed, strikingly different from the Karns encountered by Witherwing and Nada up until this time. Fortunately the valley became more thickly wooded as one climbed higher up its flanks, its basin, where the road ran, seeming to have been cleared for cultivation, though what was grown could not be seen at this season. Small pens of animals—usually the horned swine that they had met in great numbers as they first approached the valley of Karn-Ingli—stood close by most of the scattered dwellings on which they looked down from the edge of the snowy forest. And one night, by the diffused milky light of a bright moon behind clouds, Witherwing slipped out of the trees and down across the open snow to such a pen, hoping to carry off a piglet as a prize. The one meager window of the farmer's hut was heavily covered, and Witherwing had already observed that these Karn farmers shut themselves in for the night and would be unlikely to emerge unless he created a particular disturbance.

Banked up along the inner wall of the pen lay an enormous horned boar with a thick coat of bristles; its breath came and went in volcanic heavings, its crooked mouth fluttering around aggressive tusks. There was no way in which Witherwing could make off with this monster, whether surreptitiously or otherwise; but behind the boar there was an opening cut into the hillside which seemed to lead into a small chamber occupied by a sow and a tasty litter —at least, the various somnolent grunts and movements from within suggested to the princely pig-thief that this was the case. Silently he slid a leg over the side of the pen and was about to plant his foot on the muddy floor when he stiffened and froze—for what had seemed to be churned then frosted mud was revealed under scrutiny as an interweaving mass of snakes such as he had observed clustering round the hot pools. Already his foot was at a lower level than the flight of the snowbird which he had seen ripped out of the air by a snake, yet he feared to make any swift or sudden effort to raise it lest this should only attract the attention of those stone-dull eyes. Slowly, without taking a breath, he began to withdraw the foot, expecting with every drumming pulse the rapid slam of one of those mud-colored heads against his leg—but even as he continued this action it dawned on him that he could not see any heads or eyes, and that this was because the snakes did not have any. Witherwing had almost stepped into a pile of the boar's food; he was glad not to have done this, for, though it held no danger of snakebite, the mangled heap was not welcoming.

"Not a good grave to have one foot in," thought Witherwing ruefully. "Still, it might have been worse—it could have been mine. And if I can crawl under lakes and fly down mountains, I can surely succeed as a pig-thief!"

With that the prince vaulted the wooden barrier at a point where he would not have to land in the snake heap and for a moment felt a boyish exhilaration at an adventure so unportentous—stealing from a small farmer who could personally offer no real threat to him. Then the boar woke up.

Not with any lazy stretching and snorting and bemused flickering of eyelashes, but with the suddenness of a snake attack. It did not lie and look at him curiously, but rather burst to its feet in the moment of waking and charged at him. Witherwing wondered whether he had merely feigned sleep—this speed was unbelievable, as the snake's had been. The bristling bulk of the creature fell on him like a meteor, catching his leg savagely with a raking blow of the horn quickly followed by an upward thrust of the tusk. Had the boar not made a slight slip in his foodpile Witherwing would certainly have been pinned at the groin to the wall and there would have been no escape. As it was, the boar thundered into the wall, splitting the thick logs, and turned with a seething fury to strike again. Instinctively Witherwing played the bird as he rose on one knee, fanning out his swan's wing and giving himself that eyeblink's extra time to launch himself over the pen wall just as the quickly recovered boar mashed the wood with his horns.

"A Hrasp among pigs!" murmured Witherwing limping off. Despite his damaged leg he could see the ironic comedy of nearly killing himself with a prank.

The noise of the affray must have been uproarious, and Witherwing must have been unconsciously expecting it when the door of the farmer's hovel opened, for he immediately curled up in the snow where he was and tried to conceal himself behind his white feathers. It might work, and he did not want to have to kill the farmer whose stock he had unheroically tried to steal.

Out of the door stumped a hunched figure wrapped in a coarse-woven cloak suggestive of poverty and hardship.

"What dunghill bastard's there, eh? I've got a stick, you know, eh, if any scabby beggar's there!" said the farmer, peering about and scratching himself for a while. "Ah, it's nobody here, you tick-ridden pox-faced bladder-bellied pig of a pig. You great stinking lump of snake-grease," he went on, addressing himself to the boar and beating the sty with his stick. "I'll ram my stick right up your fungoid . . . Ah, what the . . . Go off to . . . I'm going back to . . ."

Muttering such complaints the farmer, bent, it seemed, with labor, shuffled back toward his door, and Witherwing felt relief at his easy escape. However, from beneath the farmer's dark hood there looked out a pair of remarkably animate glittering eyes, quite out of key with the external appearance and manner of the figure, and they were reading the meaning of the tracks in the snow which Witherwing, in all his haste, was not considering.

The upright man who took off his cloak when again shut inside the hovel was no coarse peasant farmer.

18

Perched on a wooden superstructure that over-topped the surrounding trees stood a fortified watchtower barbed at the corners with antlers of the great deer of the Upper Lands. It commanded a wide view across the valley, along which ran the road to Karn-Ingli, growing hourly more frequented, and out over the country beyond the valley to where the ice-peaks reared into the sky. But, however effective the watchtower might have been in discerning the approach of an army, it was not difficult for Nada and Witherwing to steal by unobserved among the trees quite close to it.

Nor was it difficult for the tall man in a farmer's cloak who was following their tracks at a discreet distance.

From time to time Witherwing climbed a snowy pine in order to keep them headed in the right direction, which was easily recognized since volumes of smoke billowed skyward from what was obviously the city of Karn-Ingli. The misadventure with the horned boar had taken place on the previous day, and it now looked as though they might reach the city before nightfall.

"Tonight I should like to sleep in a solid wooden house again," said the prince. "But there can hardly be a city in the world large enough or mixed enough for us to lose ourselves in."

"I have heard that Karn-Ingli surpasses all other towns in its size," Nada observed. "We can have little idea of it from the raiding parties that get to the Flatlands—they are small affairs in the lives of the Karns."

"Why is it that they don't simply overrun the Flatlands and make them their own, since they are so many?"

"They could—perhaps one day they will—but they have no need to. This valley gives them space enough and their population hardly grows at all. You can see how rich the land is too, even though it's under snow now. The ground itself gives them warmth in the coldest times. If this land ever really lets them down, then we shall all sink under them."

Witherwing became abstracted.

"What am I doing here?" he said to himself.

In fact, despite all the great and painful efforts he had made, he was waiting for events to resolve themselves before him rather than initiating action. It was a temptation now to abandon caution by announcing his presence and so provide himself with some tangible and immediate aims. Witherwing still could not entirely banish from his mind the seemingly ingrained idea that his quest would conform to the outlines of a bardic tale—it *must* have an object, its end *would* be clear and grand, even if tragic.

An almost palpable sense of Kryll's chuckling ironic presence came over Witherwing as an ice-sharp thought intruded:

178

"If I go down to that road now I shall be killed, and that will be that: it will all add up to nothing."

This kept the prince from rashly betraying himself before he had some further knowledge of Karn-Ingli but he was well enough aware that death might come to him in hundreds of ways before he achieved anything. He wondered how far Kryll might be controlling the situation, if at all, whether Hrasp-the-Hunter was just waiting for Witherwing to drop into his power.

Lost in such thoughts, which was like walking on thin ice, Witherwing passed with Nada from the pines into woods which resembled the giant trees which the prince knew from the far borders of Tum-Barlum. Here the trees were not quite so enormous, but their branches spread extensively, often dipping under their own weight to the ground and re-emerging like an independent growth, and now the forest floor grew darker, for the thickly entwining upper limbs of the trees had created another floor high above, where it seemed possible there would be a population of spidery tree-dwellers. Witherwing also recognized an occasional monstrous fungus, suspiciously like the flesh-eating giants he had known in his homeland. He and Nada took special care not to touch the bark of any tree where it could possibly be avoided. There was no climbing up these trees to check the direction, and the atmosphere had become decidedly gloomy and oppressive by the time a lightening of the air ahead indicated the thinning of the trees.

The woods ended with welcome and dramatic suddenness and a smooth snow-covered bank ran steeply down from Witherwing and Nada where they stopped, dazzled at the bright expanse of the

179

valley with the smoking city of Karn-Ingli spread as
on a huge white sheet. To their right stood a small
mound on top of which was a frosted tangle of
boughs glowing in the level evening sunlight. The
world seemed calm and unthreatening for a moment
and Witherwing walked slowly to the mound and
climbed up into the twined framework, while Nada
wandered quietly in the opposite direction. It was
impossible to say how far this structure was the nat
ural growth of branches and how far it was man
made, so perfect was the balance between organ
ic and architectural form. Witherwing assumed that
it had begun as a building which, left untended
had conspired in its decay with the vegetation to
create an object which reached after a beauty be
yond both the natural and the manufactured, and as
soon as he stepped inside he sensed that this was
enchanted ground. Strangely, it seemed familiar
though the feeling could not be attached to remem
bered experience. Peace flowed into this place. H
looked down on Karn-Ingli through an arched open
ing framed by delicately serpentine branches bright
with a blossom of snow and ice that appeared
touched with living fire. The world held its breath
and the city below rose like a dream, its steep-ga
bled wooden buildings mounting at their highest t
be tipped with the same fire. Many of the structure
were painted in bright reds and greens and covered
with carvings on a scale beyond anything in Tun
Barlum, and spiky ornaments, imitating the ubiqui
tous antler, fretted the intricate roofscape. Smok
hung like a blessing over Karn-Ingli while a murmur
like the distant sea wafted up from its streets. With
erwing could make out some tiny human figure
but none of them moved; it was as if they were dee

in reverie. Perhaps Witherwing's dream within the enchanted frame had simply stopped time, had made a picture out of the world. He was looking out on an unchanging ideal of harmony, and there was a veiled suggestion of a forgotten former existence, which was far removed from what he had expected of Karn-Ingli. However, such contradictions did not come to trouble him, for the vision he saw now wiped out all tracks and breathed a formless tranquility and resolution. Fire and ice, blossom in winter, a glorious city of the imagination—Witherwing did nothing, and nothing was left undone. Time hung like the sun-brightened smoke.

Violently the vision was ripped away. Clubs hammered down the airy structure of boughs, swords sliced through the enchanted arch, and Witherwing was gripped and bound and a knife was put to his throat before he could find heart to resist.

"Mother Ice! But that was a damn easy thing."

"Damn right! I thought this was a warrior we were after, but it's a pocky little bird. I'll poke the bastard in the beak, I will, and pluck a few of his frigging feathers. How do you like that, you dung-grubber?"

But Witherwing paid little heed to the painful minor cruelties that the half dozen or so Karn warriors visited on him. Far more shocking was the destruction of the world where he had stood just before the attack. In place of the magical woven canopy there were now only a few broken branches, some bent and jagged strips of metal, and a variety of ugly nameless fragments scattered over the trodden snow of the mound. The city itself had lost all its ideal quality with the removal of the arched frame, its smoke had turned black and swirling, its carvings

and ornaments, which had been a cause for wonder, a few moments ago, now seemed violent, cruel
and barbarous, and with the stirring of the wind
came a sharp and rotten breath from tight-packed
houses. The vast rectangular enclosure of Karn-Ingl
with its complex grid of streets had seemed a
miracle of design, but now Witherwing could see
only the triumph of a harsh and iron will clamping
a life-denying order upon a nation.

"Come on you frigging bird, *march!* Or you'l
get a horn up your ass. *Hup-hup!*"

A bone-tipped spear was rammed bruisingly in
to Witherwing's back, a fist threw his head forward
and his bound hand was jerked out in front, forcing
him to stumble forward in the midst of the Karns
who had fallen into an unpleasant march rhythn
that seemed to be done with ghostly slowness and
yet took them along at a considerable rate, so long
were the strides.

"*Hup-hup-hup, HA! Hup-hup-hup, HA! Hup*
. . . Move along now poxbrains! Keep in time
Hup . . ."

Pulled from the front and prodded from be
hind, Prince Witherwing was hustled toward the
antler-crowned great gate of Karn-Ingli.

When Nada heard the sounds of the Karn attack
ers she had already strayed a long way along the
margin of the wood, and as she turned to run back
tall cloaked figure detached itself from a tree nearb
as if he had been stalking her for a long time. .
strong hand snaked over her shoulder and presse
on her mouth, and though she dipped swiftly at the
knees, biting on the muzzling hand at the sam
time, she found herself firmly grasped. She wa
about to hurl herself and her assailant backwar

when she realized that he was hissing urgently in her ear as a swimmer might in that of a panic-stricken drowning man.

"Just don't make a noise! I'm not one of the Karns and I don't want to hurt you, I'm one of Kryll's friends, one of yours, of Witherwing's. Only keep quiet. We can't help him now, not just now, but we can once he's inside the city. They're not going to kill him yet, but they'd probably kill all of us if we tried to get him back now, and anyway don't you see that this way he gets right inside the city without any creeping around . . ."

Nada relaxed and nodded her head so that she was released, but instead of turning passively to this unpromisingly introduced "friend" she leapt from him, whirling round to face him and snatching a knife from her belt at the same time. Crouching slightly she weaved around him with her knife-hand undulating ominously like a snake's head.

He was a tall man, dark with a shaved face, and wearing, beneath his dirty cloak, clothes of a much finer quality, studded and buckled with bright metal. Nada's threatening posture discomposed him not at all.

"You don't have to do that, I shan't harm you. On the contrary, I want to give you some help, since, at a few removes, I'm really responsible for your being here in the first place. I've been expecting you for some time, and following you for a while too. Your friend obliged me by dropping in for a pig yesterday, but I fear it was not a great success. In some ways he hasn't done too well today either, but it's not so bad as you and he might imagine, and with me to help you it will probably work positively to your advantage . . ."

Nada lowered her knife.

"Explain," she said.

She sensed that he was telling the truth, but was not sure that she liked his tone, which was aloof and superior; so she added:

"I might still kill you."

19

Like the garish mouth of a beast, Karn-Ingli's horned gateway reared over Prince Witherwing and he was swallowed by the murmuring city. Grinning demons, haughty eagles with savage claws, monumental swine and stags were carved swarming up the pillars of the torchlit gate in colors violently bright, and barbarous gongs announced the arrival of the captive. The scene flashed confusingly before Witherwing, who was never allowed fully to regain his balance by the marching Karn warriors. Just inside the walls two trees flanking the head of the street revealed themselves dangling not large fruit gourds, as it had seemed at first, but wind-turning skulls, some white and fleshless, others in various states of decomposition. On roadside poles at intervals bodies were impaled cruelly on antlers, and, as the first handful of offal scraped from the street by a ragged Karn citizen slapped wetly on his neck, Witherwing wearily and disapassionately pictured himself pinned up like this with his wing outspread. Soon he was blinded by the dirt thrown at him in this way, so that he stumbled and fell in the churned mess of the street while the populace jeered and the warrior class, with their staves and spears which the cowed glances of the people showed were no mere ornaments of office, looked on in supercilious silence. Not once did the Karn warriors falter in the unnerving rhythm of their march, and when he could not walk, the prince was simply dragged like a worthless lump through the slush. Gradually the procession became amplified by torch-bearing soldiers marching in ranks and singing in time to the tramp of their feet about blood, fire and sweat, and, more especially, about death—about the somber wonder of death, the dark welcome of death, the joy of violence that climaxes in death, death the great mother whose arms enfold the world.

For a moment before he was tumbled through a heavy dark doorway, Witherwing's mud-spattered eyes cleared enough for him to catch sight of a broad flight of stone steps leading up to the highest and most ornamented of Karn-Ingli's bristling buildings. It burned with a fierce red in the torchlight—a fitting backdrop for Hrasp-the-Hunter who stood at the top of the steps, a head and more higher than any of the warriors who attended him. Witherwing just saw the antlered head thrown back and heard above the jeers of the crowd and singing of the soldiers the deep rumble of Hrasp's mocking and triumphant laugh. Then he was buffeted down dark and narrow corridors where the sound of many feet grew thunderous till he was thrown on his face through a small space on which a door immediately and violently slammed. Muffled, the sound of feet receded, and there followed a silence so profound that the prince thought he had gone deaf. The cell door had crashed with implacable finality. Raising his head he saw dimly that the massive door had no locks, handles or latches on the inside, while the fast dying light that fell upon it came from a wrist-narrow chute in the opposite wall. It was a light that trickled miserably like green water down a drain. He was alone in the sepulchral silence, and no effort of his could ever release him from this sordid space which seemed to offer nothing worth exploring. Still, Witherwing propped himself upon his elbows and dazedly scanned his prison. He sniffed the air—it was stale and cold; he scraped at the mud floor with his fingernails; he groaned, rolled on to his back, and stared up till the contours of the earthy ceiling came darkly into focus; he rolled back and crawled painfully to the wall, against which he pressed his palm, trying in vain to draw himself up into a standing position. Falling back, Witherwing began a tentative investigation of his body with his hand in an attempt to discover what damage had been done; but his heart was not in it, and his movements were vague and ineffectual.

"Am I real?" the gestures seemed to be asking. "What is the substance of this nightmare?"

As Witherwing's hand hovered abstractedly over his bruised ribs, it encountered an unfamiliar object in a pocket—not a weapon, certainly, for all those had been plucked from him. His mind mapped out the dark continents of the low ceiling while the hand, seeming quite unconnected with it, went on exploring, and in the stillness of his prison the prince was suddenly shocked to hear, plain and near at hand, Kryll's inscrutable and mocking laugh.

"Heh-heh-heh!"

It was like rising from the green depths of the lake and bursting into the air in a shower of scattered silver when Witherwing realized that Kryll's chuckle was merely his own tired mind's way of waking him to the fact that his hand knew what it had found. He remembered the limp-covered book fluttering like a broken moth toward him down Kryll's bottomless well, and it almost seemed that he was just now catching the book as he drew it out to look at it. For a long time he lay staring at the object held a few inches from his eyes. It was bound in a soft velvety leather of faded green, which was probably once embossed with gold leaf; it was thin, small, and delicate, like a young girl dying, and opening it was like turning a wasted corpse. The pages were brittle and yellow, and who could tell how many ages had passed before they pitched down Kryll's well and made the impossible journey through the eternal snows?

Very soon there was no light at all. The book dropped on to Witherwing's chest and rose and fell with the breathing of his heavy and exhausted sleep.

Stiff with cold Witherwing awoke long after with a splash of icy light on his face, so that when he opened his eyes he found himself looking up through the chute to a dismayingly distant patch of white sky—a blank page. As this image occurred to him, Witherwing fumbled at his chest and then on the cold earthen floor at his side where Kryll's book had fallen during the night. Again he held the volume too close to his eyes to focus with precision. One could not have told from his expression how far he was really conscious of his setting or of the object he dangled tremblingly over his face, and it seemed that he had called up strength from places painfully deep and could do nothing now but wait for it. Warm blood stirred in him at length and hurt blossomed where he had been bruised by his captors. He found that he could sit up and that the dizziness he felt when he had done so soon passed away. Now the light cut a thin line through the cell and glared starkly on the ancient pages of the book.

It was meaningless to him.

Witherwing had learnt to read a little, unlike most of his brothers, but this volume was not in the script of the bards of Tum-Barlum and the language seemed utterly foreign. At first . . . But gradually, as he stared at the page in the profound silence of his prison, that disquieting sense of a dream existence which he could not quite recall, that feeling of a shadow seen sometimes in the corner of the eye but never presenting itself to a direct gaze crept over him like strange music, and his flesh literally crawled. Here he was again treading into dark empty air where he had expected solid ground; it was as if mountains melted, flowed like a wave, and burst like a puff of dust that could be held in the palm of the hand. He did not understand the words, but they began to engage in a mysterious ritual with his mind, not making sense exactly, but communicating like the dance of some alien people. Words made gestures that plucked at him under sense; the language became a kind of rhythm rather than a meaning to him.

> Cast the bantling on the rocks,
> Suckle him with the she-wolf's teat;
> Wintered with the hawk and fox,
> Power and speed be hands and feet.

There was a pulse in these words that seemed his own. Witherwing realised that in his mind he was making sounds from the apparently foreign symbols, and sense trickled through some of those sounds. What was it called, this book?

It had a noble sound to it, but across the title in faded ink some words were scrawled which Witherwing knew instinctively to be in Kryll's hand, and though there was no deciphering the writing he also somehow knew that Kryll had rendered futile the grandeur of the simple title; he had beaten once upon it and found it hollow, and this scrawl was the bitter victory of his ironic chuckle, which seemed to sound again in the still dungeon.

But the book spoke to Witherwing like music that boomed from giant pipes:

> *Trust thyself: every heart vibrates to that iron string. Accept the place the divine providence has found for you, the society of your contemporaries, the connection of events. Great men have always done so, and confided themselves childlike to the genius of their age, betraying their perception that the absolutely trustworthy was seated at their heart, working through their hands, predominating in all their being. And we are now men, and must accept in the highest mind the same transcendent destiny; and not minors and invalids in the protected corner, not cowards fleeing before a revolution, but guides, redeemers, and benefactors, obeying the Almighty effort, and advancing on Chaos and the Dark.*

"*And we are now men . . .*" Witherwing shook out his caked and bedraggled feathers and pondered the strange-sounding music. He turned to the last page:

> *Nothing can bring you peace but yourself. Nothing can bring you peace but the triumph of principles.*

Then came in large and noble letters: "END." Followed by more of Kryll's writing—this time deliberate and legible, without irony, suggestive of glacial bleakness:

> What's to be done after the end? This man's words were never true—now less than ever. We should have forseen that things go dribbling on after the last days. Self!—that's ceased to have a meaning. It's all finished, and it's probably not worth asking what's to be done. All those selves—they just did for themselves.

Witherwing's beard was white with frost, his bruised forehead wrinkled by thought which could not win through to the certain answer for which it searched. His eyes rose from the yellowed page to the tiny square of blank sky and round to his prison door, which was also blank. Except, he now noticed with shock, for a single eye, which was staring down at him through a small aperture set high in the door. How long had he been silently observed? Anger leaped up in him at this violation. The shifting of the eyeball, the blink of its lid—these seemed obscene to Witherwing who raged to prick the eye like a boil. But before he made a move he thought better of it, knowing he would merely waste himself and gratify his captors by useless shows of resistance and frustration. There was no corner in the cell that would provide effective cover from the swivelling eye, so the prince stayed where he was and feigned unawareness.

In a distant cell someone began to scream repeatedly and unrestrainedly. Abruptly the noise ceased.

A book.

A square of light.

An eye.

And a breathing bundle of rags and feathers.

What did it mean, that the end had already happened?

The inexplicable music of those opening words rolled like a wave:

> *Cast the bantling on the rocks,*
> *Suckle him with the she-wolf's teat;*
> *Wintered with the hawk and fox,*
> *Power and speed be hands and feet.*

20

Ranks of torches burned thick and red along the floor of the wedge-shaped valley at its sharp end. The steep walls of ice sweated and glared while smoke curled up and wreathed in the air with a yellowish steam that rose from a woundlike slit of warm mud round which the torches clustered. And in this mud a ghostlike dance was being executed by a body of tall warriors in horned helmets; its rhythm was implacable and sinister, and the somber precision of the dancers was more deadly and suggestive of violence than any wildly abandoned dance could be. Sounds of sucking and squelching made a grotesque accompaniment to the chant of the dancers and spectators and to the deep pulsation of drums and gongs. Witherwing looked down from a great height and saw this already monstrous ritual distorted by distance and the capricious play of shadows. At first it seemed to his tired and straining eyes that the Karns were dancing in blood, until he recalled the hot muddy fissures he had encountered on first coming into this country—but then he thought that he saw mud-covered bodies of dying men being trampled beneath the feet of the dancers. With the steam, smoke, shadows, and the surrounding night he could not be certain, but every so often, just as he had persuaded himself that this was a ghastly illusion, a muddy arm or head would seem to rise protestingly only to be stamped down. Gradually the words of the rumbling invocation became distinguishable to Witherwing:

> *This is the dance to the end of time*
> *Splitting life's grape, spilling blood like wine*
> *Time dies away with a trampling joy*
> *Fierce as fire, fast as a boy*
> *This is the dance that feels life out*
> *Feels it through feet, hears the blood shout*
> *This is the dance to the end of time*
> *Wades in the heart's hot blood like wine*
> *This is the dance to the end of time*
> *Earth's blood, body's blood, joy of the tread*
> *Which tramples the heart, feels it out till it's dead*
> *The dance that untangles the fibers of life*
> *That jumps like a flame and stabs like a knife*
> *MOTHER ICE, MOTHER ICE! we are back at*
>   *your womb*
> *MOTHER ICE, MOTHER ICE! for your sons make*
>   *room.*

Witherwing himself was at the summit of a narrow vertical ice-fall which closed the end of the valley and from which its steep walls fanned out. He was pinned to a stout Y-shaped wooden frame embedded firmly in the ice, his arm being roped to one upper beam and his outstretched wing nailed to the other. In fact, the nailing had done little harm, and the prince could have torn his wing away from the wood with the loss of only a few feathers, but at the moment such a gesture could serve no purpose so he remained to all appearance firmly pinioned. At the ankles he was numbingly bound, and his feet tried vainly to rest on the projection just too small for them. The familiar antler ornaments of Karn-Ingli sprouted from the top of each arm of the wooden frame. He was the prize prisoner on display. On either side of him blazed huge torches, by which stood the two Karn warriors who had set him in his place and who were now almost in a state of trance, so hard were they concentrating on the weird ritual taking place far below.

From down in the valley the eye would be caught immediately by the winged figure, small with distance but godlike in his elevation, picked out in fiery light against the night sky. Then, if the eye travelled down the vast entwined columns of ice, it might just have been able to pick out, about one-third of the way down, the mouth of a cavern; and to call it a mouth was hardly metaphorical, as icicles exactly like teeth were ranged inside the lips. Perhaps the ceremony below was directed toward making this mouth utter.

Where he hung, Witherwing could see right down the valley, straight and symmetrical as if it had been gouged out at a stroke by some super-human instrument, to the spiky contours of the great city of the Karns. Immediately below him the muddy—perhaps bloody—dance went on flanked by files of chanting warriors with flaming brands. At right angles to these, further rows of armed men spread across the valley, facing the dance and the ice-fall, and beyond there seethed a lightless rabble possibly stretching as far back as the city itself.

It was with a certain lofty and exhausted calm that Witherwing contemplated the scene beneath him, rendered the more estranged by his weariness and hunger. He turned his head up to the sky where, in rifts of cloud deeper and wider than the valley he overlooked, the cold stars glistened in their infinite distances, and it seemed as if some fluid from him passed upward through his gaze and sped along those cloud canyons on to a plain of midnight blue and utter calm—from which he turned again to the fiery mashing of the earth in which the Karns indulged. They seemed so small and far away, as if, in the light of that starry plain, they had already ceased to exist; indeed, whether they had ever existed at all seemed a question of no significance.

Except that tonight they intended to kill Witherwing.

Death rose to him like a scent. Below all was womanless, brutal, senseless—mud and blood. No doubt the Karns saw splendor in the regularity and precision of their ranks and movements, the exact orchestration of a body of men so that they moved like one man, or one mechanism, at the word of command. Command was what they loved, laid like a whip upon them for every move they made—to them it was a caress. Some bargain had been struck with pain, so all these men had given themselves up to her on condition that she would grant them order in return; and pain's subjects did not care whether they inflicted or felt, for in her rituals the fulfillment was the same. Had they lost themselves in pain? Or did they find themselves in her?

"All those selves—they just did for themselves."

Kryll's words would seem to suggest that it would be worth paying a price to escape the self, but Witherwing, so recently lost among the stars, would have wanted a deeper acquaintance with what self was in him before he bargained it away. On the other hand, if these muddy and mechanical Karns had found and were expressing their essential humanity down there, then Witherwing was ready to pay the price of death so that he would not have to express his; no lesser price would have been acceptable.

Like long grasses swept by wind the ranks of soldiers swayed and parted. It was a neat division, leading up towards the mud-cut where the dancers suddenly halted, and up the new-formed path Witherwing watched the passage of a huge pair of antlers, the focus of all attention. Several warriors led out a white snowbull to the edge of the dancers' red patch and for a moment the antlers paused before the bull. Then Hrasp's head was down and, with a clash easily audible where Witherwing hung, he had engaged horns with the animal, at which moment a great roar surged up from all the warriors; it was an exultant bellow that bound them all together to encourage their master in this death-lock. Unbelievably, the bull began to falter backward and the level of the Karns' roaring rose to a frenzy; the tight control of movement started to fray at the edges of the ranks where hysterical shifts were taking place. As soon as the bull's back legs floundered on the red mud Hrasp, still pushing forward mightily with his antlers, drove a blade repeatedly into the animal's throat and rammed its head into the mud. It collapsed to a sound from the Karn warriors that was more like wailing than cheering, so far were they gone in their excitement; it was hoarse, cracked, hot, and unhealthy.

Hrasp stepped back, raising his bloodstained arms.

At once the gongs brayed out again and the dance began anew, now with more overt violence, but still at a deliberate pace, all keeping time. And now it was unmistakably grisly, for the object of the dance appeared to be to trample out what vestiges of life still persisted in the snowbull. There was a horrifying literalness in the words of the chant that sang of the "dance that feels life out." For a few of the warriors this sacrifice proved overwhelming, so that they broke ranks and fought through to the dance where, removing what clothes they could, they attempted to join in that sinister stamping. The dancers continued to execute their steps while the frenzied intruders were clubbed and left where they fell, sharing the fate of the bull in the mire of the dancing-ground. Bodies and mud churned together.

> *MOTHER ICE, MOTHER ICE! we are back at your*
> *   womb*
> *MOTHER ICE, MOTHER ICE! for your sons make*
> *   room.*

There was no longer a clear demarcation between warriors and rabble further down the valley, though whether it was an orgy of killing, rape, or just dancing that was now taking place in that area could not be clearly seen. Pain never kept a bargain to the letter. And her servants either never learned or never cared.

Witherwing remembered the manfish that he had watched Hrasp murder; there came back to him the desperate appeal of its manlike eyes, its agonizing moan, and the tears that had rolled down its face. The prince roused himself, breathed deeply, then cried out in a voice that carried far down the valley, penetrating the din of drums, gongs, and chanting:

"Hrasp! You are in love with extinction, and you want nothing more than to grasp your own heart and squeeze it dry. You are less than a blind worm —it's dry already. You can do nothing. You are already dead, you and your dung-treading slaves."

All fell suddenly still below. Hrasp's head slowly turned up till he stared mockingly at Witherwing. After a despising pause his laughter rumbled and re-echoed among the high walls of ice.

"The bird squeaks!" he called. "But, you luck-less albatross, you are wrong about death. It is you who are dead. I have an arrow here that tells me so, and he is unerring; he will find you out and get to know you deeply. Then there are many that envy him and shall follow him in swarms."

Here Hrasp signalled with the hand which had plucked a bone shaft from his quiver, and four ranks of archers, two each side of the dancers, raised their bows toward the prince.

"You've flown a little high. High enough to make a nice offering to Mother Ice."

At the mention of Mother Ice a shout swelled up from the ranks of Karns that, to Witherwing, seemed infinitely desolate. When silence came again Hrasp notched the arrow on to the string of his powerful bow, and Witherwing looked down on a sea of upturned faces where the light was a fierce red and the shadow, absolute black.

Much of the face of the ice-fall was lost in dark-ness, so that it appeared from below almost as if the white-winged prisoner floated high in the air.

Hrasp's bowstring grew taut.

All at once the pinioned wing flashed free and in one of those moments that seem to hold time in suspense the crowd in the valley watched a single white feather, quite clear despite distance and flick-ering flame, drift on a breath of wind out into the night and disappear. Witherwing arched his body and shouted in a tone that might have been either agonized or exultant:

"Nada!"

In the same moment both the Karn warriors at the top of the ice-fall toppled over the edge without a cry but with sharp spears in their backs, and before an arrow could be loosed the torches had followed the sentries down into the crowded valley, leaving Witherwing shrouded in darkness. Arrows began to clatter around him on the ice, but most went wildly astray. He had seen Nada as she had dealt with the soldier on his right; there had not been time to take in what had been done on his left. But when he felt the ropes cut away from his arm and feet he did not hesitate or waste time on questions. He felt for Nada's strong fingers, briefly clutched her hand, breathed in the welcome fragrance of her dark hair, and was ready to fall in with whatever she directed.

"We have a rope round your scaffold," said Nada. "We'll climb down that till we reach a cave in the ice, and once we're inside they won't follow us. Are you fit enough?"

"Yes."

"The prince in the middle," a man's voice instructed. "I'll come last."

Nada slipped over the edge and, with one ankle looped into the rope, began to descend hand over hand. The stranger tied a length of rope round Witherwing's waist and put the other end round his own so that he bore some of the prince's weight when they went down, which they did after Nada had entered the cave. As Witherwing and the stranger climbed lower, they were sighted by the Karns, but it was not difficult to shield their bodies among the columns of ice thick as tree trunks, and anyway as the escapers neared the mouth of the cave the archers below seemed to lose heart, seemed almost to panic. The ceremony was disintegrating into chaos. Looking down on the Karns from between the icicle teeth at the front of the cave, Witherwing reflected that whatever it was these people trusted to give them order would always let them down, would always turn upon themselves. Perhaps, as he had said to Hrasp, that was what they really wanted. Their city itself expressed something like this—at first it appeared to a newcomer as a triumph of order and control to build on such a scale, but it did not take long before the spiked violence of Karn-Ingli communicated itself through its architecture. Then the city wore the look not so much of an ordered rising of buildings as of a savage upheaval, as if something had broken upon an immovable object and been deflected in splinters.

Witherwing looked up once more at the shifting cloud chasms and the calm stars, and then turned to face the darkness of the cave.

"I might have known," he said aloud, but for no one's benefit except his own. "After the high places, the pits and dungeons. It's becoming quite a habit with me." He turned to the shadowy stranger. "You're not Kryll, unless you've worked one of your wonders. But you must be something to do with him. Pardon my lack of courtliness; I'm sure I'm most grateful, but a sacrifice who survives tends to feel lightheaded."

"It's a discerning lightheadedness, Prince," said the unruffled figure, who turned out to be no stranger at all, for Witherwing now recognized the voice of Hess. "Yes, I know Kryll well enough. I know you. You know me and I suppose I got you here and that, in some ways, I'm responsible for what you are. But that's another story, and it will be concerning us soon enough as it is."

"This is Hess," put in Nada. "He has a strange tale, much of which I don't understand, but he has helped us in many ways already and now promises to bring your quest to fulfilment if you will do your part."

"I know Hess," said Witherwing slowly, "and perhaps I should kill him. I think this may be *his* quest. He brought us here and if he's helped us, it's to use us."

"Well, I can't profess to love you like a mother in your world," Hess observed, "though there are different degrees of that sort of regard, as you might know. But I do have an interest in you and you shouldn't despise being used a little bit. Think how sad it would be never to be used—to be useless, in fact. I don't say 'trust me implicitly'; it'll be altogether more exciting if we keep some tension in the atmosphere and I want you to be on your guard. But I won't pin you up as Hrasp did and you may find a way of using me, too. There *are* things to be gained by all of us. *I'm having fun.*"

The ugly note of glee in this last assertion jarred on Witherwing. He remembered Hess wriggling and squealing with pleasure at the bloody sports which Harand had presented in Tum-Barlum.

"No doubt 'my quest' will mean that we follow this dark cave. As I said, I am well practiced in these journeys. Let's be on our way."

"There need be no haste," said Hess, "for we shall not be followed here. First we should give some explanations to each other. And, I expect, some food."

So Witherwing ate and told bitterly of his capture three days before, of his imprisonment, and of long periods of brutal questioning by captors who really had nothing to ask and who had no interest in what he answered, but who relished the ritual of bullying. As he had been dragged into the city of Karn-Ingli, so he had been dragged out of it and pinned high in the icy air where he had been at the time of his rescue.

"I have heard tree-men singing of Masters and Makers, I have felt incomprehensible songs reaching for me from Kryll's books, and now I have heard violent men raise their voices to Mother Ice. I have had visions of a player of magical games, dreams of flight and pale faces. What have these songs and dreams to do with me? Perhaps more important, what have they to do with you?"

"Ah, you are a seeker indeed! Who could have expected so much?" exclaimed Hess. "You fight and you dream. A perfect quester. And you shall reach some answers."

But what Witherwing now heard from Hess grew to be as inexplicable and alienating as his dreams. He still could not fathom to what people this tall, cool man belonged, nor why he should want to use or help Nada or the prince himself. Hess told his side of Witherwing's pig-stealing attempt, of how he had followed him and Nada up to the point of his capture, and of the planning and execution of his liberation. Witherwing also understood that Hess maintained some sort of contact with Kryll, who in turn kept watch on Tum-Barlum and the Flatlands partly through the medium of the unobtrusive For-

203

est Folk. However, Hess and Kryll were not cooperating in the same game. These things Witherwing could comprehend, yet some of Hess's speech was as obscure as the words that the prince had read in his dungeon—and it had almost as powerful an effect upon his imagination too. Hess seemed to be speaking not just to another people, but of another order of beings, of which he himself was perhaps one, with awesome powers, divine control and invulnerability. But though Hess talked with familiarity of this hidden and miraculous world, something in his manner suggested that he did not wish to be identified too closely with it. All this was dazzle and confusion rather than revelation to Witherwing, but he sensed that such was the intention of Hess, so he abandoned himself to receiving impressions rather than reason and facts. Witherwing saw again the image he had once received from Hutt of the godlike meditative player who turned manic in the pursuit of his complex, form-changing game. And there flowed into his mind his dream experience of flight —the wooded borderland and his moated tower rushing away from him at a dizzying speed, the Flatlands spreading like a table far below. And then the hair rising at the back of his neck, the growing dread. . . .

Hess produced a beam of light without kindling flame and directed it down the cave.

"I'm a master and maker and player," he finished. "And I've not gone down to sleep or barbarized myself, as so many have. Well, this must be rather high-flying, I know. But I've explained some of the mechanics of my part; the rest—the revelation—will be best done by those it involves more closely. Because, you see, I want to lay it on as a surprise for them, or, rather, for her. I'm going to re-unite you."

He flashed the beam to indicate that they should begin to walk.

"With your stepmother."

21

Hess passed to Witherwing the sword and dagger which he had recovered from the devastated structure at the wood's end where the prince had been overcome by the Karns.

"It's not that we'll be going into the situation where you'll be using them, you understand," said Hess. "But I want to set you up properly—make the right sort of impression for our surprise visit."

"I might still kill you," laughed Nada to Hess. And she meant it. "You and your magic beams."

By now Hess no longer required this magic beam, so he flicked off his light. For here was no ordinary cave—it was a far greater wonder than Kryll's deep cylinders into the earth. Overhead flowed a continuous stream of white light under which the three progressed quickly on a smooth black floor that muffled sound. The walls of the tunnel were white with silver rails running along the top and bottom and vertical silver strips at regular intervals. At the top of each strip an animate gray box hummed like a beehive and turned an unwinking eye upon the three travellers. There was no dirt to be seen, no cracks in the walls, none of the animals that might be expected under the earth, and the air, which had grown gradually warmer, showed no signs of losing its freshness. A low rushing sound, like that of a distant waterfall, neither increased nor diminished as they advanced.

For the most part they walked in silence. Witherwing had already had his outburst after Hess had made the announcement about their imminent meeting with the Queen of Dread. Hess had told the prince that he need have no fear; the confrontation was not set up to harm him.

"Fear!" Witherwing had snorted scornfully. "What has my fear to do with this? It is my anger that you should consider. Fear would not keep me from that witch. But you!—what makes you think that I am yours to toy with? I am not on strings, I don't have stops for you to play tunes upon. I am not any man's property, not even my rescuer's. By contempt you will earn contempt. And maybe your own death."

Hess had seemed genuinely penitent; it had showed through his words, even though he could never quite throw off the habits of irony.

It's my misfortune, prince," he had said. "I have as much to learn through you as you through me. There is too much of the controller in me still, too much of the magister. Whatever you are, I am less than you, so pardon me. Our quests are similar."

Ahead of them the tunnel glowed with red light. Hess stepped unhesitatingly into it, though to Witherwing and Nada it looked dangerously hot. The whole of Hess's body was now surrounded by an aura of bright pink luminosity, and he turned and smiled at his companions.

"This just cleans us up a little for inside," he said. "It's nothing sinister, and you won't feel much. Step in."

They did, and the novelty of the experience caused them to linger for a while in this area. They raised their hands to their faces, delighted at the sparkling outline that clung to them; they pressed their radiant faces together in an embrace and laughed. Apart from a slight tingling feeling all over the body, such as one feels when in particularly good health, the glow had only a visual effect, but this was so pleasing that it was hard to see how one's spirits could fail to be raised by such a bath in light. Witherwing drew out his sword and was close to awestruck by the magical appearance of the blade with its lambent flushed nimbus. It was like something from a bardic tale.

The river of white light which ran along the ceiling looked a little more matter of fact when Witherwing and Nada emerged from their roseate irradiation, but there was no time for feelings of anti-climax, for they saw that the tunnel ended in a black wall ahead. Gray boxes continued to turn and stare at them as they advanced toward the dead end.

"Don't worry," said Hess, turning round. "We go through."

"Remember, Hess," Witherwing replied, "that we are not worried. Perhaps you have cause to worry, or to fear. Rivers of light and glowing bodies are surely wonders, but we have seen strange sights before . . ."

"And I might *still* kill you," added Nada, smiling.

"My friends, it's my misfortune. Again I beg your pardon. I shall learn. It's just my way of speaking. And now, we go through."

Hess stood facing the blank white wall and merely pronounced his name, at which a tiny black hole appeared in the center of the wall and rapidly enlarged while the white surface folded itself away in a series of spiralling petals. Witherwing and Nada passed through where Hess beckoned and the fish-eye door closed quickly and silently behind them, leaving them in profound darkness. Hess spoke his name again and shortly it seemed like sunrise all around them as light swam up from no particular source. The amazement of Witherwing and Nada grew while visibility increased; at first because they had entered not a room, but an enormous cavern, and then because it was not so much a cavern as a world in itself. It was impossible to distinguish the confines of this world, for, in all its terrifying symmetry and precision, it stretched away from them in every direction save behind. Its height could not be determined as it remained in obscurity even after the light had intensified to the strength of bright sunshine at the lower levels. In front of them extended an endless nave of evenly lit white and silver, while on either side ever more complex perspectives of arches receded, all equally illuminated. Witherwing had not stood long before he imagined a sky above him and ceased to think of the forms he saw as artifacts. The scale of all this was so stupendous that Hess, had it been of any interest to him, could have capitalized on Witherwing's wonder; but he did not. Witherwing and Nada could make nothing of the forms they saw. Karn-Ingli had been new and surprising to them, but they could recognize its grotesque carvings and elaborate roofscapes as the work of men, just as the High Hall of Tum-Barlum, for all its grandeur, could be seen to be the work of hands—many hands, and skilled hands, but the hands of men nevertheless. With the carvings of Tum-Barlum the eye could rest on details, could go on from observation to observation, but here in this white and silver world everything seemed distant, and no single comprehensive article could hold the attention. Witherwing's grip upon reality began to loosen more than it had ever done among the estranging heights of the ice-peaks.

Hess came to the rescue by directing them to look at a particular object.

"I want you first to look below us, there to the left, at the rows of frames, boxes. Or on the right, if you like, they're on both sides of the central aisle. Do you see? Can you see what's in them?"

Witherwing and Nada strained their eyes, but it was so hard to concentrate in this vast space; it involved a great effort of will to narrow down one's vision, and just as it seemed one was about to succeed in isolating a detail a sense of measureless scale invaded the perception like a sudden rush of snow-blindness. Eventually, however, Hess's patient explanations had some success.

"They look," said the prince, "like . . . bodies."

"And right you are, prince! They *are* bodies. You might say that when you're looking at them you're looking at God. What a dreary thought. These are the controllers, the magisters, all plugged into dreamland. It'll all be explained very soon now. Over here," he pointed to a section of the wall behind him, "I'm going to get an image of those bodies projected. It will be a picture, that's all, but it will take us closer to them."

Hess began turning a small dial on the wall and then spoke his name again. Immediately the wall rippled with light, and Witherwing and Nada felt as if they were in motion, floating at an unvarying speed above the huge sleepers.

"The image is magnified," Hess remarked. "And it's moving—you're not."

The bodies were very pale and entirely without hair, men and women; they seemed flawless too, utterly unblemished in a way that was grotesque to Witherwing. They lay motionless in clear bluish bubbles on beds of spotless white, and thin flexible pipes of red and yellow ran from bottles, fixed by some invisible means above the bubbles, into the arms and flanks of the bodies where long silver needles were taped to the skin. Silver discs sprouting wires were attached to each gleaming dome or skull, and, though it was impossible not to think that there was life in these arrangements, not an eyelid flickered, not a lung drew in breath. A seemingly endless succession of pale beings passed across the screen. The effect on Nada and Witherwing was eventually hypnotic; it was as if they were in an underwater world.

"Give me Reine," said Hess to the screen.

Body after body floated across it. Then at last the movement ceased, and one woman, indistinguishable, it seemed, from the others, took all their attention.

"Come back, Reine," said Hess in a flat and controlled voice. "This is Hess. I'm asking for an awakening."

For a while nothing happened, but then Witherwing saw the red tubes which ran into the woman's body flatten and grow taut. Slowly the ivory pallor of her skin was replaced by a slight flush; her lips, her nipples began to redden, though it seemed likely that by the standards of Witherwing and Nada she would remain a markedly pale-skinned creature. The needle attached to the yellow tube withdrew itself from her side and a hitherto unseen fitting of the bed on which she lay reached up and stripped the tape from her skin. This was followed by the barest quiver of lips and nostrils at the first inhalation of air which, as it was exhaled, carried a drawn-out whispered word.

"*Leave . . .*"

As if this were sport Hess suddenly recovered his thorny irony.

"Come along, Mother Ice! For your sons make room! Here's one I've brought to see you. An awakening please, dear goddess. You have obligations to the world."

There was a flicker of her lashless eyelids, then again that ghostly whisper, the words slow and painfully halting.

"*Leave us . . . no more . . . over . . .*"

"Over, eh! Over the moon with joy—I expect that's it. Here we come now. *Up*, Reine!"

The silver discs lifted themselves and peeled away from her skull, her breasts heaved with a full magnificence, and the red pipes with their needles left her as the yellow one had. The blue transparent bubble opened like a lotus while the white bed began to raise the waking woman to a sitting position. Larger and larger on the screen grew her head; it seemed to be looming out at them. Suddenly there was almost unbearable tension, sensed by all three of the watchers. Before them was a huge pale head, its red lips just about to part, which they did as if with a soundless laugh that might have registered anything, at the same moment that the eyes opened glittering like icy stars.

Witherwing's sword slashed at the giant head which, hairless or not he had at last recognized with horror as belonging to the Queen of Dread. His strokes were ineffective.

"No, that won't serve you any purpose," said Hess gently. "I regret the shock to you. But even if that were not just an image, it wouldn't work. She would just print herself up again as she fancied, and you would find yourself used up in most unpleasant ways. Come, learn a little more first. You probably have the advantage here, though, you don't know it. However, that advantage, for the moment anyway, is certainly not your sword."

The unscathed image on the wall looked out at them and spoke:

"Leave us, Hess. Why are you here again? I thought you had left to turn wild. That you'd tricked yourself out by now like a Hrasp and chopped yourself around till you became a brute. We have all gone down, and we hadn't thought of coming back this time. You should join us, or leave. I am tired of the game."

"Dear Reine," exclaimed Hess, "I tired of the game long ago, which is why I left for the outside."

"No. You are still playing, Hess. What have you brought?"

"Mother Ice, I have brought you your sacrifice. Queen of Dread, I give you your stepson. Reine, I present you with one of the playthings you have made. Just a little something you printed up once."

Witherwing sensed evil in Hess's irony. He did not understand the meaning of his words to the Queen, or of hers to him, but he felt that they were heavy with menace for him; he was being treated as a thing, not as a man.

"I forget," said the weary red-lipped Queen. "And I have no desire to recall anything. You know it's all recorded. If you can still get in here, then you know you have a right to consult whatever records you wish. Please do that, for I intend to go down. There is nothing—*nothing*—to keep you here save mischief. Why do you persist? Everyone else has gone down. There is nothing left."

"That may be so . . ." began Hess, but Witherwing burst angrily into the exchange.

"There's a *world* left, you witch!" he cried.

"What is that?" asked the Queen of Hess after a pause; she was still cold and distant, but there was at least a germ of interest now.

"I've explained to you," said Hess. "Sacrifice, son, thing."

Puzzlement furrowed the domed brow of the Queen. Obviously she still could not remember, but it looked as though she might want to.

"Bring it down," she said; and quietly, to herself, "So many games."

"Come . . ." said Hess, but he got no further before Witherwing had a dagger to his throat, just on the point of puncturing the skin.

"*Things* will not rise up and stab you for what you call them," roared the prince. "But I will do that! And I will make that witch's throat red as her lips. Then let the wound call me a thing."

"Quite," observed Hess, unperturbed. "Your pardon. I wouldn't dream of calling you a thing. Merely irony at her expense. Come now, let's go down to her. You've nothing to lose by this, and possibly that whole world you mentioned is all to gain."

"Nada comes, too."

"Of course."

They walked over to a translucent cylinder of wide radius which reached far up into the darkness and down through what could be endless series of floors below. Witherwing and Nada had obviously both resolved inwardly not to hesitate over each new wonder, and they stepped without question through

214

an opening and on to the black disc which plugged the cylinder at the level of their feet. Slowly and smoothly they floated down, and in the miraculous suspension saw infinitely mystifying changes of perspective among the white and silver forms around them. The level at which they had first entered was a mountain's height away by the time their descent came to an end at a gesture from Hess. Now they trod out on to a white path in continuous motion like a stream, and, looking to his left, Witherwing perceived that they were passing close by the bodies in their clear bubbles that had appeared on the screen above. In fact, this was still confusingly like looking at the screen, since they made no effort and yet were in motion. The Queen had not left her bed, but because she was sitting up she could be seen far down the line as Hess, Witherwing, and Nada slowly approached in a silence as uncanny as the unchanging rate of their progress. When they were close enough for a reasonably detailed scrutiny she turned her glittering eyes upon them and it began to seem that some magnetism in her glare was implacably sucking them to her. The path stopped as they drew level with her. There were no greetings. Witherwing found her nakedness and hairlessness disconcerting, but she herself was contemptuously composed, looking over Witherwing and Nada as if they were inhuman curiosities.

"So many games," she said to herself, looking at the winged prince. "I made this! It's very fine. Perhaps I should switch something into me to clear things up a little; it's all so dim, and I'd lost interest. Did I tell you, Hess, that we hadn't planned on coming back?"

"Reine dear, you did," he assured the Queen. "But don't switch anything into you. Let's be *primi-*

215

tive. After all, that's what you think I left you for. This, dear, is Prince Witherwing. I'm sure you must be his dream lady. Witherwing, this is Reine, whom you know, a little dramatically, as the Queen of Dread, and whom you have already in spirit greeted when you saw her above."

"Witherwing. Witherwing," said the Queen reflectively. "And so he is too! How fine! It must, of course, be recent. I think, Witherwing, I knew your father."

"I think, madam," answered the prince, "that you were his wife."

"You're right. What was his name and where was it?"

"He is King Rumi and his kingdom is Tum-Barlum."

"Tum-Barlum! I remember making that before Rumi's time. And Rumi—I felt I had to try him out, since it was strange to find such fertility in afterdays. And, as you yourself bear witness, I had a taste for creative play then; it's gone now. Your wing I like. I'm glad we brought that along to Tum-Barlum. I can't remember how it was."

"Your gifts to Tum-Barlum," hissed Witherwing, "were death and sterility."

"I think you had death and sterility before you saw me. Besides, you and such places need death and sterility or you become a bore."

Here, politic, Hess stepped in to prevent Witherwing applying his sword to the reality as he had applied it to the image.

"Perhaps," he said, "since, in several manners of speaking, this is your long-lost son that I have brought back to you, and since he has borne all kinds of trouble—such as might excite even you—to be here, and since a multifarious variety of hints have snowed upon him without anyone, including myself, explaining anything to him—taking, I say, all these things into consideration, perhaps you owe him an account of his history. Or even an account of History generally."

"History!" exclaimed the Queen. "That has never been our interest here. You with the wing, look where I point. What do you see?"

Witherwing's eyes followed her finger.

"I find it hard to say what it is I see," he said. "All that is here is strange to me, so that I don't have the words, and I cannot encompass the vastness with a look."

"Well, wingie," the naked Queen continued, "those are files you see. Those are countless miles of files, and every mile contains countless years recorded on file, and nothing passes that is not so filed. What is passing at this moment will go on file, and the act of recording will itself be noted and filed. Now *that* is history. It has very little interest for me, but there it is. I would even maintain, certainly until I was awakened by the person who brought you here, that it is finished anyway. But I cannot deny that the filing goes on."

In the interest of discovering something at last Witherwing suppressed his anger. But his hopes were not sanguine, for he noticed that as the Queen grew more fully awake, so she was the more given to the irony which he had already encountered in Kryll and in Hess.

"Queen, you have spoken of after-days," he said. "And when I was with Kryll he too . . ."

"Kryll! That old bastard bibliophile!" laughed Reine. "He left before you, Hess. What did he do? Crawl off to make love to books?"

"No," said Hess in the same tone as the Queen.

"He turned from books to lizards; made love to the lizards and burned the books. He took over some workings from one of the war-eras and decided to transform himself into Merlin. It's a fairly straightforward temptation for our kind. But let's return to our history now. Prince, put your question again."

⌡ "I want to know what are the after-days. After *what*?"

"What is the answer to your question?" mused the Queen. "For it surely presupposes an answer, which will not be the one I shall give; it's not an open inquiry. What you want to hear about is a single identifiable point in time, an event, a catastrophe, after which nothing could ever be the same again. Well, nothing ever is. I've told you, Witherwing, that I have no interest in history—sometimes I think I have no belief in it—but I can assure you it does not work as your question presupposes. There is not one event or catastrophe that will explain what you want to know: there is an endless, tedious, bloody and bitter succession of such events. Not a sudden sweeping death, but millions upon millions of sudden sweeping deaths, countless boring mutations of them. Remember those files. I could hold in my hand," she stretched it out, as if she were doing so, "the tape of one year, and on it place another, and another, and so on till I held perhaps a quarter of a century. You look through at the files, and you see not the palm of my hand, but an area as big as Tum-Barlum. It's that many events and catastrophes you want to know about. You could not count the years since the world ended as anything except the game of us whom you now see. Whom you see because *you* have been made as a part of our play—a minute fraction of a handful.

——"I printed that wing on you. It replaced a withered arm, and it looks fine, it looks dashing. But don't inquire any further. It won't help you and I probably won't remember. It might traumatize you, which, in other circumstances, I could have been interested to observe. I know you things are sensitive about our origins, however little you understand them. It's best for you to invent them for yourselves. Have you encountered the furbeast or the manfish?"

"Both."

"Do you know why it is that they affect you as they do?"

"It seemed like enchantment to me."

"No," said the Queen. "It's because they are your brothers. That's all. And you have a deep fear of being brother to a slobbering furbeast, of being just a step away from that. We might have made the furbeast and the manfish, I can't remember, or they might have evolved from the boring millions of mutations of death before the game. Probably they are a result of both.

"I think I meant to do something with Tum-Barlum, but I can't remember what it was. I've just let it alone. Your father must be old, and your brothers were tedious material to work on, so I more or less let them be. I hadn't planned to return, from this going down . . . but I've probably told you that."

"But this makes a mockery of life!" shouted Witherwing, growing more appalled the more he heard.

"Yes, I suppose it does," continued the Queen evenly. "If you mean that it has afforded us some amusement."

"How can this amuse me? How can your wicked games with the lives of others amuse me?"

"You misunderstand me." The Queen was unruffled still. "I did not include you when I spoke of 'us,' and nor do we interfere with the lives of others, for we have appropriated them—they are ours. Things are owned by whoever fully controls them. That's axiomatic.

"Not that we're always concerned with full control," she went on, as if to herself. "It's often more interesting to do a bit of dabbling, then withdraw, perhaps go down, and then maybe come back to see what's happened. Sometimes one forgets, as I forgot you. Or another of us might have taken a hand with the material and given it an unexpected twist. It would be all in the files, should one care to consult them, but the game doesn't demand that."

"How long have you been doing this?" asked Witherwing, whose world now seemed a bauble.

"I have tried to explain to you that such scale is beyond your comprehension, for a couple of generations is hoary antiquity to you. And time means little to us, which is why, presumably, we are not drawn to history. Too all intents and purposes we've transcended time. We have a self-regenerating technology to serve us, though we are probably less interested in technology than in history—we lean more to the abstract. We can print ourselves afresh whenever we care to. We . . . Talking of printing, you might like to see me in my Queen of Dread hair, eh? Just wait."

The Queen's bed flattened out again and the clear blue dome arched over her recumbent body. A great silver cup came up at the back of her head and enclosed her skull. She spoke a few words that could not be heard outside her covering.

Hess nudged Witherwing and put an arm round Nada.

"She's warming to it. I knew she would. But there must be more to come. I want some real *drama!* Watch her now."

The dome folded away and the Queen was

raised smiling to a sitting position again. Then the silver cup withdrew behind her and a musky cloud of raven hair tumbled over her white shoulders and perfect breasts.

"Just the head for now," she laughed. "I might treat you to some pubic hair later on. If you're like your father . . ." Her voice trailed meditatively away.

"We're an abstract people here, but lust is amusing to me," the Queen resumed. "At its inception our order was well nigh exclusively abstract in its bent. I think. It'll be filed anyway. The great game began as something entirely cerebral, when we'd achieved the technology which freed us from the world that had ended. But the scope of the game naturally widened, and we dabbled with what was really an aftermath anyway. Perhaps we thought of something ambitious, like a new Creation! I know we got rid of an awful lot of stuff so we could re-stock on a big scale, but I can't really remember. It'll all be on file, and it doesn't matter."

"God, God, God!" screamed Witherwing. "Why have I been brought here? What have I, and all this, got to do with Hrasp-the-Hunter, or mad fantasies of glowing stones?"

"Well, as for God, in a way that could be said to be me," said the Queen calmly, lifting her hair with her hands so that it tickled her breasts. "And the glowing stones are not quite fantasies I assure you. Then Hrasp: you've probably gathered that, like Hess and your friend Kryll, he was once one of us, the magisters. He was foolish to leave, that goes without saying; but he toyed with himself dangerously and irrevocably, as Hess and Kryll may not have done. And since then I suspect that some of us have worked on him, involved him in our games because he had ceased to be a magister and degenerated into a brute. Interesting subject. I haven't kept up on Karn-Ingli much since my spell as Mother Ice. I wonder if we observe them as closely as we used to do."

"I think not, Reine," interjected Hess. "Your stepson was captured by the Karns in one of the old recording centers."

"Ah yes," said the Queen. "We fitted up some obsolete temples for that, I recall. A picturesque combination, mystical technology. Anyway, young Wingaling, I'm afraid I don't know why you're here or what you have to do with Hrasp. I'll happily show you the Valley of the Glowing Stones, since I'm sure it's very clever of you to have got here. But I didn't bring you here. I don't think. Hess did. It must be recorded. I suppose I could check it. What a bore!"

At a motion from her hand the cuplike silver helmet closed over her head again and she spoke softly and quickly into it. The flat-toned reply came back to her immediately, though the words could not be distinguished except by herself.

"Well, Wingding," said his bright-eyed stepmother when she emerged again, "it appears that I did have some plans for you, though I wouldn't have bothered if Hess hadn't delivered you. I printed that wing on you partly to involve you in a game with Hrasp. Kryll worked on the Hrasp game a little before he went, which was long before your birth. So did you, Hess; I knew you were still playing when you came back this time, though you pretend to reject us.

"As for you and Hrasp, wingie, it seems my idea was to pit you against each other. As I said, I've neglected Tum-Barlum, so I haven't brought you up as a killer—which I meant to do—and Hrasp *is* a killer, most wonderfully ferocious, and he does have the advantage of having once been a magister . . .

Still, since we are here, I intend to reinstate the game. Let us have a little killing.

"But first, let me show you my garden—the Valley of the Glowing Stones."

22

The Queen of Dread sprouted pubic hair before the eyes of Witherwing, Nada, and Hess. She simply lay back and, beneath the new-closed clear dome, she was surrounded with a radiance not unlike that which had entranced Witherwing and Nada in the tunnel that had led them to this world. They watched the growth, like accelerated cress, of delicious silky curls forming an airy fluff on the swell of her mound and down each side of her dark fold, while a barely visible delicate line pointed up toward her navel. At the same time the skin of her whole body underwent a subtle change as the lightest down seemed to settle upon her, just enough to soften her previously over-sharp outline. It was a grotesque experience for Witherwing, who was both repelled and aroused with dark pleasure by this process and this perfect body.

Her thin red lips were fixed in a passionately triumphant smile directed at the prince when she returned to them.

"I knew you'd like it," she said, slipping straight on to her naked body a suddenly materialized, sweeping robe that Witherwing remembered from his childhood. Neither she nor the robe had aged in the slightest. She spoke three words into the air: "Reine. Two lifts." And almost at once there was a flashing in the air and two globes hovered above them.

"Let's go and see how my garden grows," said the Queen lightly. She turned to Witherwing: "If you do go back to Tum-Barlum you're welcome to take some blooms along with you. I don't think they did much good last time, but they will impress people."

"It's what they are expecting in Tum-Barlum, Reine," said Hess. "The prospect of a little power, however ill-defined and even if it's a deathly power, sets them all a-going. Or rather, it sets this prince a-going while the hungry ones who commissioned him sit and wait to consume what fruit he might pluck."

The globes descended where they stood, opening to reveal seats for two in each.

"Wingaling, you come with me," said the Queen, seating herself in the nearest of the globes. "The girl goes with Hess."

Nada smiled at Witherwing and fingered the short but powerful bone bow slung over her shoulder. The prince smiled back and nodded. Then they sat where they were directed. Like the bubbles that enclosed the prostrated bodies of the magisters the globes sealed in both pairs and with no more than a gentle hiss whipped them smoothly and swiftly into the air and across the vast central nave of the magisters' underworld. Unerringly they slotted themselves, one after the other, into a glassy cylindrical column like the one by which Nada, Witherwing, and Hess had descended to the Queen. Once inside, the globes catapulted upward into darkness where they shone like speeding moons. After an indeterminate ascent they suddenly shot out into daylight and hovered at the height of two tall trees above the ground.

"My valley garden," announced the Queen.

When Witherwing's eyes had adjusted to the light and the situation he saw that they were floating above a bowl-shaped valley ringed by dark hills which on the sides which sloped inward were free from snow, though at their summits and on their outer slopes the snow had settled. It was difficult to see the bottom of the valley, for it glowed, shimmered, and seemed to shift with multi-colored lights. At one moment it seemed fluid, a foaming sea of glistering color, at another like a hard bed of crystal splinters, and there were numberless gradations between these extremes. In a dazzling dance of points of light, colors for which he had no name collided, blended, burst apart before Witherwing's astounded gaze: vermilion, scarlet, crimson, carmine, ruby, garnet, rose, carbuncle, cinnabar, cochineal, emerald malachite, beryl, aquamarine, cadium, saffron, topaz, gold, amethyst, violet, cobalt, indigo, sapphire turquoise, lapis lazuli, cerulean, ochre—all surged together in rippling irridescence, in bright shafts, sparks, and stippled clouds, in prismatic whorls and jewelled showers.

"This is enchantment!" breathed Witherwing at last.

"Enchanting, certainly," concurred the Queen. "But not exactly magic. In fact, it's just like any other garden—you spread it with dung and you get your growth. Well, to be strictly accurate, you're looking at the dung now; this is a sort of manure-as-an-end-in-itself garden."

"But are not these the glowing stones?"

"Yes indeed. But that doesn't alter what I've said. This is a lovely waste land, a valley perilous: look at the hillsides." They were bare and lifeless, as if they had been irremediably seared. "I filled this

226

valley with waste, when we still produced waste—we don't now, it all goes back to our stock-pot. And this is a garden of poisonous flowers that could eat your world away. If your people try to use these stones for power they will rot like cheese. I've seen it happen, for I used to play with these. Poor Rumi! I was most anxious to meet a father of seven in a dwindling world; but I soon burned that out of him.

"Well," she continued, "this is the right place to climax a quest. Look at the hills again:

> . . . those two hills on the right
> Crouched like two bulls locked horn in horn in fight;
> While to the left, a tall scalped mountain.

You might ask Kryll about that, if you ever see him again."

The hills were just as she described them, though they did not seem to be sculpted—they looked as organic as clouds that sometimes bear accidental but striking resemblances to animals or other forms.

The Queen gestured over the lighted panel before her and the globe made a sudden drop till it all but touched the glowing stones below.

"A limited exposure is not going to harm you much," she said to Witherwing in a dismissively matter of fact tone. "Especially since I've worked on you in the past. I see that the Karns have kept to their privilege of installing a priest-gardener here. He might even be your guide if he hasn't crumbled entirely away."

Witherwing stepped out of the globe when it opened for him. Then he stood and looked intently at the Queen, who remained inside.

"Was that poetry you spoke to me—about the hills like bulls?"

"Yes."

"I learned some poetry when I was in a dungeon. This is it:

Cast the bantling on the rocks,
Suckle him with the she-wolf's teat;
Wintered with the hawk and fox,
Power and speed be hands and feet.

There followed an intense silence during which Witherwing and the Queen stared at each other hard till it seemed that her glittering eyes clouded, a which she sealed the globe and sped upward Witherwing, left on the hot and dazzling rocks tha hummed ominously, turned to meet the Karn gardener.

At first he thought it must be a trick of the kaleidoscopic light. But it wasn't. Where he had expected a Karn man he saw something like a large jittering gray thistle running with nacreous lumpy butter.

"Welcome. This way," it croaked and pointed with some part of itself.

Witherwing vomited.

"Come," cackled the nodding thistle-thing which presumably had been a man when it first came to this valley. Witherwing stumbed after over a variegated jewel floor of unbelievable magnificence.

The bewildering electric glare of color at Witherwing's feet gave way all at once to black rock, bare and dull. He looked up to find that his grisly guide had led him to the base of the cleft where the two bull-like hills met head on, and, though confusing flecks still darted across his vision, he thought that he saw horns just at the point where the heads of the fancied bulls were locked.

A deep rumbling laugh told him that this was the place. He still could not see Hrasp-the-Hunter clearly, but he stared up at the branching antlers etched against the white sky and drew out his sword with grim deliberation. Inwardly he was putting aside his weakness; if he survived he would pay a terrible price for this effort, but if it were not made there would be even less chance of his remaining alive—which would mean no chance.

The Queen hovered above, looking down from her transparent globe at the developing conflict. On a hill not far away stood Hess and Nada, the latter with her bow held ready for use.

"I meet with the killer of children again," shouted Witherwing. "But this is the last time, Hrasp, because I shall kill you now. And I shall be able to do it because I have on my side your deepest desire. Death is the gift you wish for from me." He threw out his wing, white and steady against the wild dazzle behind him. "I am the angel of Death."

There was a pause like that which preceded Witherwing's parting from the Queen of Dread. Then Hrasp began to laugh again, a mocking, self-congratulatory roar.

"This is famous, birdman, famous! The taunt, the insult, before the battle. The conventions are an endless delight to me. Oh, how successful I have been since I left the Order and turned my game to earnest."

Did he at this point throw a knowing glance at Hess? The look of a conspirator? Witherwing could not be sure, but he hoped that Nada would remain suspicious. Hrasp began to stalk down threateningly toward the prince, while the decayed gardener of the glowing stones fled back into the bright cancerous beauty of his domain.

"Yes, Witherwing," Hrasp was saying in a low voice as he advanced, "I am enamored of death, but I have him with me. Look carefully and you will see him at my antlers' ends, and he is an insistent lover of flesh and wants to be up inside yours. Watch him now. *Watch!*"

Witherwing saw that Hrasp's great horns were tipped with metal that looked as though it could deliver a rapier slash. He could not help looking at them just as Hrasp had told him to, and that nearly cost him his life before he even gave a stroke. For Hrasp, having directed his opponent's attention above his head, hurled a dart with swinging force at Witherwing's chest. The prince jerked aside and turned his body so that the missile would pass across him, but he moved neither far nor fast enough to prevent a wound being furrowed along his breast before the dart clattered down among the glowing stones.

"First blood. *I might even drink it*," hissed the horned giant.

Witherwing knew that, however much Hrasp could wound him with his weapons, his intent was to kill him with his antlers. There must be some way of using this certainty to his advantage. As a speculation he pretended that his wound had damaged him seriously and so staggered back with his arm pressed against him and rotating it to stimulate the blood-flow into something a little more dramatic. His sword wavered up past his wing shoulder, apparently ineffective. Hrasp snorted like a bull and burst down on Witherwing with volcanic ferocity. At the last

230

moment he lowered his head to gore the wounded prince, at which Witherwing abandoned his charade, swept to his left so that Hrasp tumbled by him, head down, at a ferocious speed. Witherwing's sword glittered with lights thrown from the glowing stones and curved down in a rainbow blur at the lowered head. It missed, catching instead Hrasp's antlers, shearing off several of the metal tips and throwing Hrasp himself face down in the Queen's garden. Without a pause Witherwing impelled himself toward his fallen enemy ready to chop his neck from behind. Instead he found himself flying convulsively through the air, his body raked by the mighty antlers that had dashed back at him when he had made his rush and then thrust him violently forward. Now began a wild and flailing ferment sending stones of myriad colors in showers through the air as Hrasp and Witherwing stumbled cursing among the stones, jabbing at each other in whatever ways they could. It was inconclusive and exhausting, and warily they began to make their way back toward the slopes of black rock. When he came within range of the rock Witherwing made a great leap accompanied by a powerful beat of his wing which swivelled him leftwards while in the air so that he landed facing Hrasp, who remained among the stones. So fast had he done this that, while Hrasp's eye was still open the wing, the prince was able to deliver a slashing blow along his upper left arm. Hrasp, though pained, answered immediately by hammering down stingingly with his sword on Witherwing's weapon, giving himself just enough time to jump to solid rock. Their swords bit spitefully at each other, leaving jagged notches in the cutting edges. Witherwing attempted his well-tried diversion of flapping his wing disconcertingly in the face of his opponent, but Hrasp was not taken in for a moment. With his left hand he snatched the wing and whirled the prince around with a sudden jerk; if Witherwing had not already weakened that arm with his earlier thrust he might well have found himself flying free through the air for the second and last time in this combat. It seemed disastrous enough as it was, for he lost his grip on his sword a the hurtled round. Hrasp roared as he heard it ringing down the slope and attempted to continue the swing of the body so that he could impale it on his horns. But he was too slow. Witherwing had snatched a dagger from his belt and as he slammed toward the antler tips, enough of which were snapped off to confuse Hrasp's judgement of which were snapped off to confuse Hrasp's judgement of distance, the prince plunged it into his monstrously powerful neck right up to the hilt.

Hrasp-the-Hunter threw down the prince like a doll and his eyes dilated with shock and fury. His mouth opened wide, emitting eventually a hoarse exclamation at which his lips turned a bright wet red. He did not fall. With towering strength he bore down upon Witherwing, making the air thrum with scorching slashes of his sword as the prince was forced to retreat weaponless up the slope—further and further away from his sword. The savage force of Hrasp's swordstrokes was unquenchable; with every step he took he thundered down another, and Witherwing knew he could not evade them indefinitely. Like some gross plug the hilt of his dagger protruded from Hrasp's bull-neck. It seemed to have done nothing except make him more formidable and implacable. The dread that Hrasp, the fallen magister, was unkillable spread like a sickness over Witherwing. The prince was now at the top of the black rock ridge while Hrasp advanced with an unappeasable sword. Behind him was a snowy precipice. Only measures of desperation were left to him, so when Hrasp's sword crashed downward the next time Witherwing, taking advantage of his superior elevation on the rock, launched himself forward at Hrasp's head, almost as if he were offering himself up as a willing sacrifice to the horns. When he landed on their ripping points Hrasp gurgled triumphantly, threw away his sword and lurched forward and up to impale his prey inextricably. It took only a couple of paces, then bodies toppled over the cliff. Hrasp's arms tightened round Witherwing, held him to the horns, so that when they fell into the snow beneath them the prince would be under the antlers and transfixed with the utmost violence at the moment of impact. He flared out his wing to create a disturbance in the air through which they fell, and, though he had not rolled the bodies over, he had withdrawn Hrasp's attention just sufficiently for him to reach round and with two fingers hook the hilt of his knife and pluck it from the giant's neck.

A terrible red rain gushed around them, drenching both and scattering itself in the air. Witherwing spread an incarnadine wing and threw himself from the horns. His rate of descent slowed as he fanned out his feathers and he watched the huge body fall below him, still pumping showers of blood through which the prince in his turn floated.

And down through this red spray there floated too the globe of the Queen of Dread, which settled alongside her battered stepson and silently opened its mouth for him.

Nada had been just about to loose an arrow into Hrasp's broad back when both he and Witherwing fell from sight. With Hess she hurried round the curving hill where they stood until they could see Hrasp's corpse in the red-sprayed snow and the prince entering Reine's globe. Nada closed her dark eyes and breathed out a long sigh of relief, lowering her bow, although the shaft remained notched on the string.

Hess dropped his normally lofty and ironic manner in an excess of glee, which seemed to Nada a cold and self-indulgent excitement.

"Oh what a game! What a *drama!* Just as I had hoped!" he squealed. "Ooh, I think I must have a pair of horns. Or no, a wing. That's what I want—a *wing*. I'll have his. Reine will let me have it now she's finished." He turned his flashing eyes on Nada. "It will be just the same for you, dear. I'll simply get him printed on me and the only difference will be an increase in power. Maybe I'll go down and be king, and you can share in games with me. You'll be a queen, and I'll . . ."

Suddenly he stopped.

Nada's arrow had bitten into his breast so deep that its feathered flight appeared merely pinned like a brooch over his heart.

"Come to Mother Ice!" said the Queen exultantly to Witherwing, casting her glittering eyes upon him and flashing a thin-lipped red smile. "That was a magnificent climax, an excellent bit of violence. And if I remember aright you will be wanting some lust after your violence. So come along, you sticky red bird."

They were suspended in the globe high over the Valley of the Glowing Stones. The Queen parted her robe from neck to toe, and offered her perfect nakedness to her stepson. He raised himself from his seat and arched his body over hers.

234

But instead of touching her he grasped a part of the light-fitting above her head and wrenched at it.

"Come now," said the Queen, "let's keep that sort of violence out of the foreplay. Besides, it's all unbreakable. You can't do anything to it."

Even as she spoke a tuft of white and silver splinters came crackling away from the inner surface of the globe in Witherwing's fist; an intricate mesh of wires was dragged out into the air. There was no humor in Reine's voice when next she spoke. A slightly metallic timber hinted at the beginning of panic.

"You can't do that! Stop it at once or I shall dispose of you, which I can easily do. You know that!"

Witherwing paid no attention, but continued to tear with his hand where he had first broken through the smooth interior of the globe. Having once cracked the surface he was able to inflict considerable damage, and now he seemed to be hauling out the entrails of the machine, which lurched drunkenly. The Queen screamed and issued an order to an unseen control:

"Reine. Remove my passenger—*at once!*"

The globe opened and what appeared to be a small shaft of lightning struck stunningly at Witherwing, knocking him out of the machine. However, he still held on to a thick rope of wires which the velocity of his fall stretched out, dragging a shower of miscellaneous fragments from the globe which, as the prince slowed his own fall by spreading his wing, plunged past him at high speed. Briefly he caught sight of the Queen's pale face screaming soundlessly, and then there came an explosion beneath him, a hot orange ball that buffeted him upward in a blast that singed his body and seared his lungs.

In the sight of a squad of Karn warriors, which had waited for Hrasp outside the hills ringing the Valley of the Glowing Stones, Witherwing hacked off the dead giant's head and held it aloft by the hair between the antlers; there was no horned helmet, the antlers sprang firm from the skull. The terrible trophy dripped on to the snow as the prince advanced on the cowering soldiers. Nada was at his side with an arrow ready to be loosed.

"I am your master!" barked Witherwing, playing his part; and the Karns stiffened respectfully at his note of brutal command. They were relieved to have someone to obey again. "Take me to your city where you shall serve me. And when I am ready you will escort me to the Flatlands. I have killed your kings and your gods—do not dare to disobey me."

The columns of soldiers marched their master back to the jagged splendour of Karn-Ingli where Witherwing cast the massive head into the dirt of the street; and the Karns accepted their new lord with servile awe.

23

Warm winds came back like a lover to the Flatlands. Clouds of white water surged down the falls from Kryll's lake and green lizards returned to bask on black rocks. Round Kryll's tower white birds flickered in buoyant gusts.

Draped with lizards Kryll sat in a deep wooden chair and brooded. Had he ever really made himself anew? Or was he still unconsciously manipulating a magisterial game? Perhaps the winged prince who had come back from Karn-Ingli had already achieved more than him; and he seemed set on going further.

"Ah well, nothing matters. Much. Time for play, I think."

There was no chuckle as he rose.

In the farthest reaches of the Flatlands a day dawned when a faint black line rimmed the horizon front of the sun and the air murmured as with bees. The lies thickened and the noise increased as the Horde swarmed on to the plain.

It was not long before news of this occurrence was brought to the worried ear of Tum-Barlum's new king, Brandyll, who felt more anxious than ever that his recently returned youngest brother should not leave the kingdom again.

Witherwing stood on the shore looking out at the gray sea while the first stars glimmered in a violet sky. Some way from him men still worked on the large wooden framework of a boat; among them, grinning hugely, labored Fish. Further off still was the cloaked figure of Nada, her tragic eyes gazing upon the waves. Slowly the prince raised his white wing in an ambiguous gesture that, in this uncertain and mysterious light, looked as though it might last for ever.

A MIND-BENDING FORAY INTO
ADVENTURE AND DANGER!

FALSE DAWN
by Chelsea Quinn Yarbro   (90-077, $1.95)

In the mountains neither of them stood a chance alone. Out of desperation, Thea, the grotesque mutant, and Evan, the mutilated pirate set off together to seek a haven . . . trusting each other because they must. A spellbinding novel of a defiant love illuminating the New Dark Ages of the 21st century.

STRANGE WINE
by Harlan Ellison   (89-489, $1.95)

Fifteen new stories from the nightside of the world by one of the most original and entertaining short-story writers in America today. Discover among these previously uncollected tales the spirits of executed Nazi war criminals, gremlins, a murderess escaped from hell, and other chilling, thought provoking tales.

TITLES BY KARL EDWARD WAGNER

BLOODSTONE
by Karl Edward Wagner   (90-139, $1.95)

Kane—the Mystic Swordsman becomes the living link with the awesome power of a vanished super-race. Now Kane, whose bloody sword has slashed and killed for the glory of other rulers can scheme to rule the Earth—himself!

DARK CRUSADE
by Karl Edward Wagner   (90-021, $1.95)

Kane—the Mystic Swordsman battles the prophet of an ancient cult of evil that began before the birth of man. Join in on this adventure as Kane commands an army against the power of primeval black sorcery for one purpose alone—He intends to rule the Earth!

DARKNESS WEAVES
by Karl Edward Wagner   (89-589, $1.95)

In this adventure Kane, the Mystic Swordsman leads the avenging forces of an island empress, a ravaged ruler bent on bitter revenge. Only he can deliver the vengeance she has devised in her knowledge of black magic and in her power to unleash the demons of the deep.

GREAT SCIENCE FICTION FROM WARNER...

A CITY IN THE NORTH
by Marta Randall (94-062, $1.75)
They are set out to discover the secrets of the dead among the ruins — and found, instead, the secret of their survival.

THE BEST OF JUDITH MERRIL
by Judith Merril (86-058, $1.25)
A collection of the best works of science fiction by the pioneering, feminist, activist author whose stories reflect penetrating studies into the psyche of the women of the future.

THOSE GENTLE VOICES
by George Alec Effinger (94-017, $1.75)
What will happen when men from Earth encounter other intelligent forms of life — a race so primitive it hadn't even discovered the spear, or fire . . . .